The Search

A Spiritual Novel

The Search

A Spiritual Novel

By

Olivia Ritz

INNER LIGHT PUBLISHERS

www.inner-light-in.com

Published by:

INNER LIGHT PUBLISHERS
www.inner-light-in.com
E-mail: innerlight.in@gmail.com

ISBN: 978-9382123187

Disclaimer: This is a work of fiction. Names, characters, places and incidents are either the product of the author's imagination or are used fictitiously, and any resemblance to any actual persons, living or dead, events, or locales is entirely coincidental.

Contents

The Land of the Immortals

In the valley nestled in the north east of the great Himalaya where the Sun shines bright on the forest of the alpines and the mist plays on the lap of the bluish green mountains, there is the ancient land of Amaravati. The word literally means the abode of the immortals. Surrounded by high mountain range, Amaravati is a sanctuary of peace and joy where the beauty of Nature creates pure magic and time flows in a leisurely pace.

The natives of this land are descendants of the noble Aryan clan— pious and happy people, thriving under the rule of King Vikram. They love and respect their noble hearted King and cherish their royal family.

People are especially fond of their motherless Princess. Queen Hema passed away when Princess Lila was only twelve. She is a beautiful young lady of twenty-two now. King Vikram did not remarry. Lila grew up under the tutelage of her grandmother, Devi Maya, who is still upright at the age of ninety.

Princess Lila has an excellent hand on Sitar. Music flows from her hands as effortlessly as the Ganges flows from the Himalaya. Her celestial music enchants one and all.

Today is the holy festival of Shiva, the deity worshipped by the Aryans. The city has been decorated with flowers and leafs of Deodar tree. Happy people, freshly bathed and scented are seen on the street, donned in colorful attires, singing and dancing on the street. Young ladies have adorned their hairs with beautiful white jasmine. Everybody is busy making their way to the temple— the great old temple, built by expert sculptors during the reign of Vikram IV, the great grandfather of the present King.

Built on the background of the Himalaya the age- old temple is a wonderful marble edifice carved in black granite. It has nicely been decorated with ghee lamps and flowers. Crowd has started pouring in. After they are done with offering their worship to Shiva, people are waiting patiently on the temple premises. There is an air of expectant exhilaration in the air.

Princess Lila will be seen to play her Sitar on the temple premise today. Every year on this holy night she plays her Sitar in the temple. A barricade has been formed around the shrine by armed guards to prohibit the common people enter the shrine while the princess is present there.

People are standing on the temple porch; some are squatting leisurely beneath the Deodar trees on the terrace. The dignitaries of the royal court are present too, along with the King. Soldiers are seen everywhere, keeping watch and maintaining order and sanctity of the place.

The light buzz in the crowd died down seeing the Princess appearing from the shrine. Joining her palms and slightly bowing her stately head to the gathering, she walked up to the small platform by the side of the shrine entrance where her Sitar was placed. Her gait was slow and dignified, her face calm and composed. In her dark navy blue Sari and pearl ornaments, she was looking sweet and gorgeous. A deep silence came over the place as soon as her fingers touched the strings.

Standing at a distance among the crowd, he was staring at the beautiful Princess in breathtaking admiration. Her incomparable grace and stunning beauty took him in awe.– – 'She is truly amazing.'— He mused inwardly. Dev is new to this city. Just a few hours back he arrived here. Seeing people rushing to the great temple of Shiva he thought something important was going on here.

He knew nothing about the festival, or the Princess performing there on the temple. In his village he used to hear people speaking highly about their beautiful princess and her wonderful musical talent. He never thought he would see her face to face from this nearness.

Dev was observing her from behind a tree among the crowds. She radiated a splendor and majesty that arouses a feeling of admiration. Her gaze was fixed far away. Dev noticed a subtle air of indifference and solitariness surrounding her oceanic eyes and faraway gaze. She was so gentle, still so beyond the common crowd.

She was playing her Sitar seemingly oblivious of herself. The rich and enchanting melody of her music filled the temple air. Dev was enamored. The air around the temple was heavy with the fragrance of sandalwood oil and champak flowers. He took a deep breath filling up his lungs.

The long journey from the village today made him tired. He didn't eat anything the whole day. But he wasn't feeling tired any more now. He was just delighted to listen to her wonderful music. He could listen to it and stare at her beautiful form the whole night. — Something said within him. Dev was both startled and ashamed at his thought.

Why would such a thought cross his mind? He chided himself. He'd always been very reserved and reticent about ladies. But the beautiful princess and her heavenly music took his heart in captivity. There is obviously nothing wrong in feeling joyous to listen to such a wonderful music. He thought in his defense.

King Vikram was sitting on the premises inside the fence along with the dignitaries of the royal court. He was feeling very proud for his daughter. But his face was clouded. A subtle restlessness was haunting him, clouding the joy in his heart. He was anxious about finding a successor to the throne.

Princess Lila's disinterest in the men of her age makes life difficult for him. He was worrying about his daughter's marriage. The Princess is different from most girls of her age. She has an inborn gift of self-possession, which makes her somewhat distant and inaccessible to most people.

She must marry a suitable boy..., one who's able to take over the throne. Someone needs to tell her this. Silly girl...! — A frown appeared on the King's forehead.

The music was over. The Princess received a standing ovation from the crowd. The King joined them too in the applause. But the worry didn't leave him. He was thinking about Prince Pratap of the neighboring kingdom — a bright young man of wit and humor. He could be the ideal choice for the Princess.

King Vijay, the King of the Pandas is a friend. Both the neighboring lands could prosper with this marriage. They are already very friendly to each other. Traders keep travelling to each other's land, exchanging goods... The King could think of no better choice for his daughter.

But her whim and fussiness came in the way of realizing his dream. The Princess met Prince Pratap on the wedding of his sister, Princess Sofia. Pratap, visibly impressed by Lila, tried hard to win her attention; but she kept herself somewhat reserved and withdrawn, which did not let the matter extend beyond the formal courtesy.

How great it would be if Prince Pratap could become his son in law! —The King left a heavy sigh. A furrow appeared on his forehead. — Pratap is a strongly built handsome young man. King Vikram doesn't find any reason why his daughter won't like this bright young man. At the rate things are going, she'd never find a husband. The King sighed again.

The courtiers were taking leave from one another, after congratulating the King for his daughter's musical talent.

After the Princess left in her carriage with her attendants and guards, King Vikram turned at his left to the Prime Minister Shyam. Shyam gently smiled gazing at him.

Shyam is a boyhood friend and playmate too. A Brahmin, devout, generous and high minded, he is a bachelor and a man of uncommon depth of character. The King deeply trusts and admires this wise friend.

Even at sixty-five, Shyam looks young and energetic. His friends regard his calm poise and cool demeanor with admiration and his enemies observe his self-possession with resentment alloyed with awe.

"Let's go to the Palace garden, Shyam." The King said. Shyam nodded his consent and in the royal carriage two friends left for the Palace garden.

They were sitting face to face. The King was reclining on a Sofa adorned with red cushions; Shyam on another one just opposite to him. King Vikram was looking visibly worried and tense. Shyam was curious, but he said nothing. He was waiting for the King to open up. In private two friends used to open their hearts to each other.

"I'm worried about Lila, you know." The King blurted out after a while.

"Why? She was really amazing today!" Shyam said. "Marvelous is her gift of music!"

"I'm worried about her future, you know." King Vikram became somber. "She needs a husband."

"But Lila should have no trouble finding a husband." Shyam said. "She's a lovely girl with a lot of charm."

King Vikram set his crown on the table and frowned. "On the outside. On the inside she's very picky."

"Don't be in a hurry, my friend." Shyam lifted his gaze and said. "Lila is different from the girls of her age, you know."

"I know, Shyam." The furrow on his forehead grew deeper. "And that makes me worry more. I want her safe, taken care of."

Shyam was aware of his friend's desire to get his daughter married to the Prince of the neighboring kingdom. If Lila were married to the Prince of the Pandas, the King would have found the peace of his mind. Nevertheless, that was not meant to be.

"The course of life doesn't always follow our mathematics, Dear friend!" Shyam sounded philosophical.

"Hmmm!" The King sighed.

"We have to wait, dear friend," Shyam said, taking up the glass of sherbet an attendant just now placed before them. He waited till the attendant departed, and leisurely took a sip in his glass enjoying the taste of the mango-sherbet.

"We should wait till we find a suitable match for her, a boy of similar temperament as hers...," he said after a while. "someone she'd love and admire."

"Wait till she grows old?" The King shrugged his shoulders setting his glass down on the table. Frustration was written on his face. "And where will you find a suitable boy for her, Shyam? She is not interested in any of our young courtiers either."

Shyam kept quiet. He had no answer to this question. There was a long silence. Two friends sat together till the evening came down in the royal garden. The full moon of April rose on the dark sky, above the branch of the shady Banyan tree. A servant came with lights lit in scented sandalwood oil and placed one on the marble table between them.

Shyam broke the long silence with a sigh.

"We've no other choice, my friend. Wait we must, if we care for her happiness." He softly said, standing up intending to take leave. "We need to wait till we find a suitable boy whom she'd like."

King Vikram nodded silently at this. His heart became heavy with care and concern for his daughter. She had lost her mother at a very young age. He could do anything to see her happy. The King's heart grew softer at this thought. Truly, she is such a gem — so tender, affectionate and uncomplaining. And incredible is her musical gift. How much does he prize seeing her play her Sitar beneath the beautiful Banyan tree! In her white Sari, she looks like a forest goddess. — The King sighed again. Shyam is right perhaps. They need to wait.

Love, Death and Immortality

In the afternoon they were strolling together on the Palace roof. The sacred temple of Shiva was visible on the mountain at a distance. Lila stood silently gazing at the temple. Suddenly she turned around. "Do you know, Bella, why Shiva the God of immortality is also known as the great Lord of death?"

Bella finds herself at her wits end to find the answer to this strange question. Sometimes Lila seems so beyond her.

"It's just how the ancient mythological stories describe Shiva, you know…" Bella falters, "I don't know the reason, Princess…"

"Princess !" Lila frowns. "Did you forget my name?"

"Slip of tongue, Dear friend…," Bella smiled sheepishly.

They walk up to the swing on the other side of the roof to sit over there.

"Where do you find these strange questions from?" Bella said again with a smile.

Lila smiled too. She mildly nudged her friend. The question didn't leave her, though. She played with the gold laced end of her pearl white silk Sari for a while.

"You know what? I've asked the royal priest too;" She said, "but his answer doesn't satisfy me."

"I guess you have to believe in what the ancient books say…" Bella said uncertainly, "They say Shiva, the lover of goddess Uma is the lord of immortality and the lord of destruction as well."

"That's what I'm asking, Bella. Why?"

Bella shrugged, not knowing what to say.

"How can a lover be the lord of death?" Lila muttered, as if speaking to herself. "Does love create or destroy?"

"Perhaps there is a relation between love, death and immortality, Lila." Bella said softly.

"Sure, there is. But what's it?"

The two of them were silent for a while.

"I can't exactly pin down what it is." Bella broke the silence. "But somehow I know love and immortality are very closely related."

Lila turned to her friend with question in her eyes.

"When you truly love someone, you get the taste of eternity, you know; suddenly everything becomes beautiful and extraordinary," Bella went on saying. "And your heart is filled with bliss for no apparent reason." There was exhilaration in her voice.

Lila smiled seeing her fervor. She was surprised too.

"When you are with your beloved," Bella said again, "time just flies away unnoticed and you feel there is no such thing as death."

Lila silently kept admiring the face of her childhood friend. Bella's face was radiant with a beautiful smile. Her cheeks were lighted with a crimson hue. Lila was observing the change of color in her face. Suddenly Bella didn't appear to be her usual self. She looked much certain, mature and confident, much more, than Lila ever knew her.

"Your point is taken." Lila paused to take a deep breath. "This ordinary existence suddenly becomes extraordinary when you fall in love, because Love itself is our blissful self— timeless and immortal."

"Sure!"

"Now I clearly see a relation between the three." Lila said casually.

"Do you? But, I don't see it," Bella was perplexed. "How can love or immortality be related to death?"

A subtle smile lighted up the face of the Princess and a sparkle passed through her deep, dark eyes.

"Let this topic rest for now, Bella," She said, throwing her hands around her friend. "First I need to know how my friend knows so much about falling in love."

Bella felt a gush of blood flushing her cheeks. She took her gaze off her friend's eyes. "Wh— what do you mean?" She gulped. "I didn't say anything extraordinary! ...I mean everybody knows what love means."

Lila didn't take her silent gaze off from the face of her friend. "Not everybody knows about love, Bella; at least not the way you know." She smiled and gently strokes her cheek. "Your face says something your words want to hide."

Bella knew she had been caught in the eyes of her friend. She took a deep breath and smiled meekly, gazing fully at her friend's eyes. "You're right. I know I should have told you this long before."

Lila was curious, but she didn't say anything.

"Som is his name." Bella said, not sure how to begin.

"Who's he?" Lila tried to remember if she knew anybody in that name.

"You've never seen him." Bella said hurriedly. "He doesn't belong to our royal folks."

"Oh? Very interesting!"

"He's an artist, a painter, you know," Bella said shyly.

Lila was astonished to know her closely guarded secret. Bella's father, Minister Ronen is arrogant and haughty, just unlike his daughter. He won't be very happy to know about his daughter's love affair.

She took the hands of her friend in hers. "How did you meet him? How long is he courting you?" She said eagerly.

Bella was jubilant to relate her love story to her most special friend. Bella met this young man in the birthday party of her cousin brother. She was impressed to see the painting he presented to her cousin as the birthday gift. Her cousin spoke highly about him. He said Som loved to paint in his spare time, whenever he gets respite from his farm work.

The boy is an orphan brought up by his childless uncle. They own a small farm house at the village Mourya, a place Bella frequently visited to see her aunt. Som and Bella felt drawn to each other at their very first encounter which turned into deep love within a short while and they started going out together.

Lila listened to her friend with rapt attention, speechless. Neither of them spoke a word. Under the azure sky, two friends sat silently clasping hands of each other, their hearts delighted to listen to the gushing breeze flowing through the forest of the pines at a distance.

Lila broke the silence after a while.

"You're fortunate, Bella." She said smiling. "You've found the love of your life."

Bella smiled shyly, saying nothing.

"But you didn't tell me how love could be related to death." She said after a while.

"You will understand it better than me, my friend."

"No. I won't, unless you make it clear." Bella said rising up from the swing. "I don't have such a sharp intuition as you have, Dear..."

"But you do have a golden heart, my friend," Lila said smiling, "and that's enough for a happy life."

"And so have you." Bella said, "The one that'll marry you would be really fortunate."

They came to the other end of the roof to see the Sun setting behind the mountain. The sky near the mountain was tinged with its crimson rays. The light of the setting Sun dancing on the pink and golden clouds created a breathtakingly beautiful scene on the horizon.

"How beautiful..." Lila softly muttered. She took a deep breath looking at a distance. Bella took her by her hand, lead her to a couch, made her seated and sat beside her.

"What is it?" Lila frowned, smiling covertly.

"Now solve the riddle for me, please." Bella smiled too. "Tell me how can there be a faintest relation between love and death, or I'll lose my sleep tonight thinking over that." "Love and death are deeply related, dear friend..." Lila said softly. "And death opens the door to immortality."

"I didn't understand", Bella said, perplexed. She was trying hard to grasp the meaning of her friend's words.

Lila smiled affectionately. "Love means death; death of the usual, old self. True love is an oceanic experience where you lose yourself. Don't you?"

"Very true." Bella gushed. "You can't remain the same. The snobbish Bella died when she fell in love with Som, the village painter..."

"There you are!" Lila said fondly playing with the fingers of her friend, "In true love, the lovers die; only Love remains."

"So true;" Bella whispered. "...love blossoms as a feeling of deep oneness."

"This is the reason, Bella, why Shiva, the ideal lover is also the destroyer." Lila smiled.

Bella kept quiet, trying to fathom the depth of her words.

"He dissolves our old ego-selves in his incomparable love so we are born in to the realm of immortal bliss." Lila said again.

"Sweet are your words, my friend!" Bella said thoughtfully. "But, they sound a bit strange and otherworldly... you know what I mean..."

"They are true, nevertheless."

"May be…, I'm not sure. I mean, what you say might be true for divine love; but it can't be true for us, ordinary mortals."

"No?"

"No. Total loss of ego is not possible in human love. How can we abandon our individuality?"

"Love is divine, Bella dear. There is no such thing as 'human love'!" Lila whispered. "Love is the signature of the divine on the mortal hearts."

A spark of light lighted her heart. "True; you know more about love than I ever knew, Lila." Bella said. "But tell me, how can we transcend our ego that lurks behind our individuality?"

"Ego is the culprit that mars many sweet relations, Bella."

"Nobody knows it better than the lovers in fight." Bella giggles, possibly recalling such a fight.

Lila joined her. She becomes serious again. "Individuality or ego — call it whatever you like — often creates such an insurmountable barrier between lovers, you know." She said in a serious note.

"So true," Bella nodded.

"Don't ever let your individuality come in the way of your love, dear friend." Lila said. "Our individuality is just an instrument, you know, through which Love flows. We just need to learn how to not obstruct the flow."

"How's that possible?" Bella looked earnest. She was learning lessons on love from her wise friend, — lessons unknown to her so far.

Lila kept silent for a moment.

"We can be a good channel of Love, Bella, when we learn to let go and let be."

"Really!"

"Yes! Love is really letting go and letting be. It's all about giving space to each other. It's all about respecting the freedom of one another...It's all about looking at things with the eyes of understanding, instead of the eyes of judgment..."

"It's all about respecting the opinion of each other, right?" Bella said catching the tune of her words.

"Yes!" Lila chuckled.

"Perhaps I understand what you mean to say, Lila." Bella said thoughtfully, "You meant to caution me that jealousy and possessiveness should never get the better of us... Right?"

Lila smiled. "You're absolutely right, my friend. Never let those poisons spoil your love."

"What a wonderful lesson on love! I'll remember your advice, my friend." Bella smiled gratefully.

"A person is like a flower, you know," Lila said softly gazing at the beautiful jasmine on the flower pot that started opening its smooth white petals in the moonlight. "Love is its fragrance. You can never possess the fragrance, you know. Try to encapsulate the fragrance, and the flower will die along with its fragrance; only the carcass will be left. That's the worst mistake people often make as they try to possess their beloved in an attempt to possess love."

Bella was delighted to learn the secret of true love. She felt her heart blossoming like a flower.

"I seem to get it now!" She said thoughtfully. "The drive to possess whom you love is an egoistic drive and, Love and ego can never exist together…"

Lila smiled. Her radiant face beamed in the moonlight. "You're absolutely right! They are just as opposite as the Sun and the shadow is." She said with a grin, "Love is oceanic, you know, which liberates the mind, while ego is like a small cage that binds and rots the relation."

Bella was fascinated by the wisdom of her friend. "I'm grateful to you, Dear friend," She whispered, "for sharing your insights."

"I wish to meet him sometime."

"He seldom leaves his farm, you know. His uncle is getting old and he depends much on him." Bella gushed. "But I'll surely see to get him come over here."

"Nobody will know; at least your dad won't know; I promise." Lila smiled.

"I'm scared." Bella said. "Just say you'll be my friend whatever happens."

Lila covered Bella's hand. "Always," she said. "I'm always your friend, just as you've been mine since the first time we met."

"But how do you know so much about love, while you keep so aloof from men?"

Lila smiled at the naïveté of her friend. She kept quiet for a moment, searching for an answer.

"It's just intuitive knowledge," She said. "You know; I'm yet to meet a man whom I could love and adore."

"I know. I'm so sorry Lila, if I've hurt you." Bella said softly pressing the hands of her friend.

"Not at all," Lila said smiling cordially, "you are the only one who knows my heart."

"But I'll eagerly wait to see the hero who can accomplish the awesome feat of winning your heart!" Bella said fondly.

Lila laughed. "Then you might have to wait forever."

"Why, Prince Pratap wasn't such a bad choice!" Bella teased her friend, knowing well that she didn't like him.

"Let me alone. If you have a crush on him, I'll send a proposal for you. But then what'll happen to poor Som?"

"No, Som is perfect for me." Bella giggled. "But I was just thinking about the Prince of Pandas… the way he wooed you in the wedding of Sofia."

"That's precisely the reason I kept away from him, you know," Lila became serious.

"I've met him too. Nice guy, but boring." Bella said, "But His Majesty would be very happy to see you married with the Prince."

"I know," Lila sighed. "But whenever men look at me with greed in their eyes that puts me off. What can I do?"

"Is it so easy to demarcate between love and lust? The line is very fine, dear."

"I agree, Bella. But you know the difference when you notice how someone makes you feel."

"Please explain..!"

"It's so obvious… doesn't need an explanation. You know it. Every woman on earth has got this feeling, I think."

"Still…, please, I want to know your thought on this."

"Every lover is kind of a worshipper, you know; a worshipper in the Temple of Love, in the shrine of wonderful oneness of heart. Hence love makes you feel divine…" Lila said taking her gaze down to her palms, "But lust makes you feel more like a commodity to be enjoyed."

"But then doesn't sex have its place in the relation of married couples?"

"Sure it has; but it should come as a by-product of love, as an urge to feeling oneness." She said. "Then it becomes a divine union. Sex without love is ugly."

"You're amazing!" Bella said hugging her friend. "I could never explain it this way."

Two friends sat together, silently holding the hands of each other, gazing at the vast panorama of the bluish green mountain range at a distance. A flock of wild swans flew over their head toward the west. A maid on errand brought the Sitar at her bidding. After checking and adjusting the strings, Lila started playing her sitar. She was playing the raga Poorvi, a raga of the dusk. The rich melody manifested the mood of the end of day.

The pure melody of her sitar was flowing through the hills and the dales, touching the earth and the sky, the river and the trees. Long past the evening Lila played her Sitar, totally oblivious of the time, and Bella sat near her, bathed in her music.

The Stranger

He was walking briskly with a cotton towel and a cotton bag on his shoulder and a brass-pot in one of his hands. Ganges was not far from his home. In spite of holding such a prominent position in the royal court, Shyam has chosen to live a modest life without much display of royal pomp and luxury. He feels content with his simple life, that to many, speaks of his courage and strength of character. With his accessible and modest profile, he can easily reach and relate to the people, and has few enemies, if any. People love their wise, courageous and kind Prime Minister.

Today is Monday. Shyam used to keep fast on the Mondays. Just before the daybreak, he decided to have a dip in the river Ganges. Ganges is sacred to the Aryans. The Aryans consider this river as the sacred flow of life itself. They regard it more as a goddess than a river.

Having a dip in the Ganges is considered an act of great merit; it washes away all sins, they say. Shyam doesn't bother with those theories. It was only a lifelong practice that made him feel good to worship Ganges and have a dip in it on special occasions.

This hour in the morning is called the Brahman-muhurta, the sacred hour of Brahman. The time is considered very auspicious for prayer and worship. Darkness started to dissipate by the time Shyam reached the bank of the holy river.

A few people were already present on the riverbank. An old ascetic was counting his prayer beads sitting on a stone. A young lad was immersed in deep meditation and two others were having their bath in the river. One of them floated a small canoe made of leaves and flowers, with an earthen lamp, lit and placed carefully in the middle. It flowed with the current, the flame of the lamp steadily dancing on the water for some time, until it disappeared under the stream.

Shyam kept his towel and the bag on the stairway and slowly climbed down with the pot tightly held in his hand. He waded through the water until the water reached his waist. He dipped his pot, filling it with water and poured the water on his head. A shiver went down through his body. The water was ice-cold. The glaciers of Himalaya melt in the summer Sun and flow downwards as the pure water of the Ganges.

After pouring a few pot-full of water, his body was seasoned with the coolness of the water. Shyam sat down for a split moment to take a dip. Then he stood up, took a dip again and did it again for a third time. His whole body felt soothed and pure, with the coolness of the water penetrating every pore of his being.

The dip in the cool water had a strange healing and refreshing effect on him. No wonder that they regard Ganges as a great purifier, he thought.

By this time, the crimson rays of the morning Sun flooded the eastern horizon to create a divine splendor on the sky.

'Om Jabakusumo sankasham…' Shyam uttered the holy Sanskrit prayer in praise of the Sun, joining his palms. 'Om, thou crimson red in color! Thou, the source of great luminosity! To thee I bow down, O harbinger of the day. Thou art the destroyer of darkness, sin and ignorance.'

Now he joined the palms of his hand and placed them in front of him to form a cup; he dipped and filled them with water. Uttering mantras of salutation to the Sun, he lowered his palms toward his fingers to pour the water down to the river. Twice more he did so, offering the water in worship to the Earth and to the Ganges itself. He mentally offered the sacred water to lord Shiva, and then to his ancestors.

When he was done with it all, Shyam stood there in the water silently for a while, admiring the beauty of the tiny wavelets on the Ganges glowing and shimmering in the rays of the morning Sun. — Down the centuries, the Aryans had worshipped the great river as a sacred manifestation of the Divine.

Shyam had seen his father and grandfather worshipping the Ganges, the Sun and the Earth. Offering homage to the Divine had never been a blind ritual for his ancestors. It was an expression of gratitude and admiration to that which holds on, supports and nourishes human life. Gratitude was a way of life for the ancient Aryans.

Shyam's grandfather passed away at ninety-eight when Shyam was only twelve. He taught him to cultivate gratitude to the Ganges, to the Earth and to the Sun. Gratitude makes the heart rich, adds beauty to life and makes the life worth living; he used to say. A half smile appeared in his lips as those thoughts of his childhood crossed his mind.

Now that his worship was over, Shyam came out of the water. He climbed up the steps and grabbed his bag to bring out a dry towel and cloths to wear. He also took out a small canoe made of the leaves of the Sal tree, flowers, matches, an earthen lamp and a small bottle filled with clarified butter. With the towel he dried himself and changed his clothes. Now he arranged flowers on the pot, placed the lamp on it, poured the butter in the lamp and ignited it striking the matches.

Carefully taking the lamp on the flower pot in his hands, he went down the steps, bent downwards and placed the lamp on the flowing stream. The current took the pot away immediately. The lamp kept dancing on the wavelets as it flowed away, but the flame continued to burn bright.

Shyam was gazing at the flame as long as he could see it. Now that it was gone, he turned back to climb up the stairs. His glance fell on the young man again. The youth was still sitting there on the stone platform, meditating. He looked relaxed and upright, with his eyes gently closed. Unkempt hairs covered the upper part of his broad white forehead, which seemed to shine with intelligence and erudition. He seemed around twenty two or so.

Shyam stared at him for a while. There was something in that face, a regality which arrested his attention. This was not a common face. His noble birth was apparent from his high brows, broad, shining forehead and elegant features. Tightly closed lips spelt of determination. The beauty of his strongly built form was admirable. As if, strength, grace and beauty mingled with each other to form his form.

An unusual curiosity grasped Shyam to find out who this young man was. He'd never seen him before. Such a distinguished appearance can't go unnoticed even in the crowd of a million people. Probably he is new to this city. Shyam silently sat on the stair at a distance from the youth, waiting for him to open his eyes.

After a while the young man opened his eyes. He did not seem to have noticed Shyam at first. His silent gaze was fixed on the Ganges. There was a subtle air of stateliness about his gesture. Shyam was silently admiring this youth and his dignified bearing. He was bent upon finding out who this man was.

Slowly, he withdrew himself and his gaze fell on Shyam. Shyam smiled and the youth smiled back.

"Are you new to this city, my friend?" asked Shyam. He did not know what prompted him to address this youth as a 'friend'. He was amazed to hear his own words.

"Yes, I'm." The boy said. Then, with a little hesitation, he asked, "Sir, do you happen to know Sage Ramanam? I've heard that he resides on the mountain at the farthest end of this city."

Sage Ramanam was a saint of repute, a simple man living in a cave on the mountain. His age, nobody knows. On festive days, devotees flock to him to hear him speak of God. Shyam admires the sage and visits him often.

"Yes, I know him. In fact, I visit him often."

"Really?" the young man was delighted; "Sir, can you please show me the way to the mountain where he lives? I have come to study with him, if he kindly accepts me as a student."

"Well, I was planning to visit him tomorrow, early in the morning. I can take you there, if you wish."

"Thank you Sir. That'd be very kind of you; but I thought, I was going to visit him today."

"As you wish; but the place is a bit far away from here. It will take you almost the whole day to reach there, if you go by foot."—

Shyam was startled again, albeit inwardly, to find himself concerned about the unknown young lad. This was strange!

"I see; then I'll better wait till tomorrow. I'll be obliged to join you tomorrow morning, Sir. Thank you." The youth humbly said.

"You said you are new to this city. Where are you staying?"

"I know nobody here. I arrived here just yesterday afternoon, Sir, and I spent the night right over there." The boy smiled, pointing to a stone bench nearby. "Today hopefully I'll find out a place."

Shyam could see through his words and smile. His nobility was apparent from his pleasing persona that radiated integrity, energy and simplicity. He felt an irresistible attraction and respectful affection toward this young lad, though he did not know him at all.

"I invite you to be a guest in my house today," Shyam said with a grin.

"Thank you for your kind invitation, Sir;" the youth said, a bit surprised. "But I'm a complete stranger to you, and you don't even know my name!"

"I guess it's not that big of an issue;" Shyam was feeling a bit embarrassed. "I'll know it now." He said smiling.

"I am Dev", said the boy, joining his palms at the centre of his chest, gracefully making a bow and said, 'Namaste'.

Shyam joined his palms too. "I am Shyam."

"I am glad to meet…" The youth paused in the middle of his sentence suddenly remembering something and gazed fully at Shyam with question in his eyes, "Sir, you are certainly not Shyam, the Prime Minister of this land. Are you?" he asked.

"Your guess is right, my young friend. I do have the fortune to serve this country as the Prime Minister," Shyam said, shifting on his feet. The Sun was growing hot. "Let's go home, Dev; come with me," he said. Dev stood up and silently followed Shyam, taking his small bag, which contained his meager possessions of a few sacred books, cloths, a cotton towel and a bamboo-flute.

On the way, neither of them spoke a word. Dev was engrossed in his thoughts. He was wondering at this strange bounty of his fortune. Just yesterday he stepped in this city, where he knew nobody; he had nothing to eat, no shelter — he slept on the riverbank beneath the sky. The little money he had was mostly spent on the road. The rest of it, he gave to the driver of the carriage who brought him here. Yesterday evening after listening to the music of the Princess at the temple he came here, drank the water of the river and fell asleep on the stone bench nearby — and today he is the guest of the Prime Minister! How strange the ways of destiny are...

When they were about to reach the Prime Minister's residence, Dev broke the silence.

"I thank you again, honorable Sir, for being so kind to me to invite me as your guest", he said.

Shyam turned to him and kept a hand on his back. "I'm happy to have you as my guest, my young friend," he said.

Dev was too surprised at the informal and cordial attitude of the Prime Minister. He had heard people speaking highly about the kindness, generosity, piety and intelligence of their Prime Minister. But this was something unimaginable.

Lost Was His World

Shyam's house was near the Palace, just adjacent to the Palace garden. Armed guards greeted them at the portico. On the inner porch, there was a beautiful statue of the propitious God Ganesha, complete with his long bended trunk, disk and hook, conferring the boon of wisdom and wealth.

A middle aged attendant came up and bowed low to them.

"Jivan, meet Dev, our new guest. Make good arrangement for his stay and take good care of him." Shyam said to him.

Then, he turned to Dev. "Dev, go with him. He'll show you your room".

The house had many foyers. The beams and walls of the hallway were carved with stories of olden time, of Ram, Sita and Hanuman, of Radha and Krishna. Rooms were decorated with beautiful pictures and portraits. Dev was led to a spacious room on the second floor. Dev looked around the room, after the attendant left. There was a bed covered with soft white sheet with blue laces at the borders. He found a small marble-top table in the corner.

Sensing a beautiful fragrance, he looked around to locate the source. It was coming from the white flowers in the vase on the table. He found a water jug and a fruit-bowl, filled with apples and grapes.

Dev was feeling very hungry, but he didn't touch the fruits. He wasn't used to take food on his own and eat, unless served. He walked up to the large window at the eastern side of the room and looked below. It faced a large garden decorated with fountains and statues. He found trees and bushes laden with fruits and flowers. Just below the window, there was a bush of the Night-queen. A large lake was seen at a distance. Dev admired the beautiful landscape.

Standing alone in that big room, suddenly he felt that strange yearning in his heart; it was back again. It felt like a strange ache, which made his heart feel hollow. Those painful memories were back again.

Dev felt like a sinking man, gasping for breath. His identity was disintegrating; his sense of self was withering away. Like a rootless weed he floated again. He stood helpless and petrified, silently bearing his inner turmoil.

He has just turned twenty-four. Life took a queer turn for him just a few days ago. He is yet to come in terms with it. He'd been thoroughly puzzled, dazed, shaky and restless since the strange flow of events that eventually brought him here.

Everything was just fine, almost perfect, before that. He took pride in his decent lineage and erudition. He was proud of his noble Brahmin lineage. He was firmly rooted in his village among his friends and kinsfolk.

Dev had been sent to the Gurukul, the house of his teacher in the neighboring village to study the Vedas when he was only six. He had the gift of a razor-sharp intellect. His phenomenal memory was envied by his friends and classmates. Within a short time he became proficient in the Vedas and adept in the grammar, arithmetic, logic, history and literature.

He took joy in studying higher philosophies and enjoyed debating on that. His intelligence, knowledge and erudition earned the admiration of his teacher, who requested Dev to assist him in his job after Dev completed his education at his twenty.

After a few years of gaining experience in teaching, Dev came back to his parent's home in their beautiful village Mandira, wishing to start his own school. Dev's father was the village chief, a Brahmin of high moral values, admired by one and all. His mother was a kind and pious woman. The goddess of wealth and the goddess of wisdom both graced the family and they enjoyed their special status in the village. Boys and girls of the village looked at Dev with admiration alloyed with awe.

He had many admiring friends, sons of the noble Brahmins. Life was flowing easy and effortless, like a happy dream.

Last year Neel, the son of an army officer, bought an estate in Mandira. Dev and Neel became fast friends. They were almost the same age, Neel a few months older than him.

A few months back, seeing Neel riding his horse, Dev suddenly had the desire to learn horse-riding. With the encouragement of his friend, Dev secretly started learning horse riding within the boundary of his friend's estate.

Born with the gifts of keen concentration and strong will power, Dev could excel in anything he put his heart on. Within a few days, he mastered the skill and within a few months, he was so adept in the art that he could break any stubborn and unbroken horse. Neel too came to admire his skill.

Dev felt enthusiastic to present his new skill before his parents. He decided to go home riding a steed.

Dev became elated at the thought of taking his parents in complete surprise. Everybody in his village would stare at him in wide-eyed wonder. He mused; and what about his mother? She would be pleasantly shocked to find her son on the horseback. It would be fun. Dev was absolutely amused at his idea.

On that fateful afternoon of his life, Neel and Dev started for Dev's home. Neel was riding a brown stallion and Dev mounted on a white breed of Kabul. They went along side by side on the village road. Men, women, boys and girls of all ages stared at them, wide-eyed in awe and wonder. Seeing them from a distance, Hema thought soldiers were coming; hurriedly she went inside the house. What made them come toward their house? She pondered in bewilderment, and kept observing them through the window.

When the horsemen came near, her surprise knew no bounds. It was Dev on the horseback! She came out on the veranda smiling, her heart filled with joy and pride. She was visibly proud of her son's accomplishment. Dev was happy too, and amused at his mother's reaction of bewilderment turned to joy.

Just before he alighted from the horseback, his father came out of his room. Seeing Dev on the horseback the color of his face changed. The old man became still and pale. Staring at Dev for a few moments he quietly retired inside his room. Dev was a bit intrigued by his father's strange and unusual behavior.

After Neel left with his horses, Dev went to meet his father. The old man was sitting quietly on a couch, his head reclined and eyes closed. He looked tired. Dev was about to leave the room, when, without opening his eyes, he called Dev near him and bade him to sit down.

Dev was feeling ill at ease for no obvious reason. However, he quietly obeyed his father. The old man opened his eyes and looked at him affectionately for a few moments.

"Are you alright, Dad"? Dev said smiling, trying to ease the unusual tension.

The old man replied not. He became grave. Dev couldn't quite get what was going on within him. The silence felt heavy on him.

"You love to ride the steeds, Dev; don't you?" He said.

Dev didn't know what to say. He was trying hard to fathom the feelings of his father. An uncanny sensation was running through him. However, he kept quiet. The old man fell silent for a moment. He certainly wasn't expecting a reply from his son. He looked tensed and anxious.

"Today I am going to tell you something, Dev...that must be told." He said again, shifting in his seat.

Dev blankly stared at his father, who looked like a stranger and his language was difficult to grasp. His father cleared his throat and broke the suffocating silence with words, which Dev was trying hard to make sense of.

"All these years I couldn't tell you this, you know... You are grown up now, and I have grown old..." His father fell silent. An unknown pressure was building up.

Dev sensed his mother silently entering the room. She sat beside the window like a statue. The air of the room was somber and tense. Dev couldn't bear it anymore. But he said nothing.

"Before I die, I must tell you this..." His father said again. "Long before you were born, we, I and your mother went on a long pilgrimage. We were visiting holy places, staying for a few days here and a few months there, as we felt like. We were childless and she was keeping vows and praying to gods, you know, for a child. Finally we reached Varanasi, the holy town of Shiva. We rented a large garden house... It was just beside the highway where the soldiers, traders and common folks of the neighboring cities used to pass by."

The old man paused for a while and closed his eyes. He seemed to browse through the pages of the long forgotten past. Dev was becoming tense and restless, for an unknown reason. A weird sensation was running through his spine.

"I think it was a Saturday...a stormy evening." His father continued. "Somebody was knocking at our gate. I bade our servants to open the gate. A man of stately appearance entered our garden on the horseback, with a woman, probably his wife, sitting behind him carrying a baby.

The lady was exquisitely beautiful, but she did not wear a veil. Nor did she put Sindur on her forehead like other married women.

However, they were wearing gorgeous dresses and jewelry, but both of them looked sick and feeble. They begged shelter from us.

The man looked like a soldier. Alighting from the horse, he started vomiting. An epidemic of Cholera had spread in the neighboring city. We heard. We had no time to ask their whereabouts; nor were they in a position to relate. Both of them were seriously ill. Both had high fever, along with the other grave symptoms of Cholera, including frequent vomiting."

His father paused to catch his breath. Dev didn't understand what this story has got to do with him. Quietly he stared at his father. The old man took a deep breath and continued.

"Your mother was busy nursing the lady and her baby. I was nursing the gentleman with the help of our servants. Again and again he tried to tell something in a feeble voice pointing at his wife and baby. His words were not clear and we didn't quite understand what he said. He took out a bag from his waist and offered it to me. It was full of gold coins. I denied accepting it…

But the man gradually sank in to a coma. I sent for a doctor, but nobody came on that stormy night. The night hours passed with us anxiously waiting at their bedsides. They lied down pale and dying. We were helpless to see them die.

The woman died late in the night and by the morning, the gentleman died too. We couldn't help them. We didn't know who they were; we didn't know where they were coming from, or where they were going.

The baby was crying. It was cold and hungry. Your mother picked it up in her bosom, caressing and comforting it. We had been childless for a long time. She needed a child and the baby needed someone to look after it. She took the baby as a blessing from the lord Shiva of Varanasi. After that strange event, we discharged our servants with ample rewards and came back to our village. We didn't feel the need to discuss it with anybody else in our village. It had almost been one and half years since we left our village. When we came back, everybody knew that we had our child by the grace of Shiva… You are that child, Dev."

Dev was staring blankly at his father. A shudder passed through his being. He could not quite believe what he was hearing. His father, who, Dev knew by now, is not his real father, cleared his throat again.

"Dev, I sent you to the Gurukul for starting your education at an early age like the other Brahmin boys, to imprint on your tender mind the conditionings of a noble Brahmin, you know." The old man said, smiling piteously.

"But you were born in the warrior caste, perhaps;" He continued. "Seed of that impression still remains within you. Your love for horse riding reminded me of that. Today when I found you on the horseback, it reminded me of that and I knew you should have been told everything."

He paused. Dev was sensing a void within his head. His voice was choked in an unknown panic. He couldn't say anything.

"You have learnt the Vedas; you have excelled in your study." The old man spoke again. "Still, the vocation of the priest or that of a teacher may not satisfy you forever. You are free to choose the course of your life. Do as you please." His father, no, his foster father, Brahmin Virbhadra paused and sighed.

Dev could hear a sob near him; it was his mother. Why was she crying? Was it because just now Dev came to know that he was not born of her? So, what? — A sigh came out of his chest. She had brought him up with such care and affection. Dev could not think her any less than his own mother.

Still this story had created a stir within him. How can he not be bothered by this, when at the age of twenty four he suddenly learns he wasn't the son of whom he so long knew as his parents?

Dev held his drooping head with his hands and sat stunned and motionless like a statue. Waves of mixed emotions were surging within his heart. Love and admiration for his parents were strong in his heart. But now that he heard this bizarre story, this love would not be the same shadow-less light, which it used to be before. A band of shadowy thoughts started haunting him. Whose son he really was? How did his real mother look like?

A subtle pang and restlessness seized his heart, and he silently walked out of the room. His pride of being an erudite Brahmin, his pride of being the able son of his father, his pride of belonging to a noble Brahmin lineage crumbled to dust. His sense of belonging was lost. Dev's world fell apart.

He could not sleep that night. He knew that the event of this evening had its toll on his parents too. Sleep didn't come to them either. The silent reaction of Dev made them afraid, worried.

In the middle of the night Dev reclining on his bed sensed drops of rainwater falling on his forehead. Astonished, he opened his eyes to find his mother silently standing near his head. It was her tears that fell on his forehead. Dev sat up and made her sit near him. Wiping her tears he said "Why are you crying, Ma? Dev is your son. You have brought him up with all your love, affection and care. Dev is eternally indebted to you." He put his hands around her to console her and sent her to sleep.

But sleep had left him. He came up to the courtyard, under the night sky. The moon was shining bright, spreading her mellow light over the earth. The sky, the stars and the clouds looked at him in somber silence.

"Dev, who are you?" The question was haunting him till he listened to the story of his strange destiny. Dev did not have an answer.

He was no longer a Brahmin; nor was he certain if he really belonged to the warrior caste. He did not know for sure who he was. He belonged to none. He had no lineage, no vocation, no social identity, nothing to hold on to.

Just a few hours ago he had everything. He had a strong sense of belonging to his parents, to his kinsfolk, to his small village, where he was brought up. He was firmly rooted among his friends and relations. Nothing has changed really, except he has heard a weird story, and that story makes him feel that he belongs to none. But this feeling was real. He felt completely rootless and lonely.

—Was his identity so fragile? Dev wondered. Was it made up of just what his parents told him? Now, because his parents told him that he was not born of them, his identity is lost. He feels rootless and alone. Are human relations so brittle? Is human identity so illusory?

What bothered him most were his father's words that were still ringing in his ears. "...The lady was exquisitely beautiful, but she did not wear a veil on her head. Nor did she put Sindur on her forehead..." Wearing a veil and Sindur, the traditional red mark on the forehead used to be the custom with the aristocratic married ladies of the land.

Why would a dignified married lady travel bare-headed? Why didn't she put the Sindur on her forehead? This must be the reason why they doubted whether the lady was indeed the wife of that man. Or, were there some other reasons too...?

Dev was tired reasoning with himself. That woman happens to be his real mother. Thinking such thoughts about her made him pained. But he could not avoid thinking. The words of Virbhadra kept ringing in his ears; "A woman, probably his wife..."

Could it be that his mother was a kept woman, a courtesan kept for entertaining that gentleman of whom he was born? Wasn't Dev a legitimate child born of the sacred marital vow? Dev was thoroughly shaken at his doubt. His whole body seemed to be despicable and sullied at the mere thought of his illegitimate birth. Dev was trembling like a falling leaf in the autumn breeze. He sat down on a bench on the yard and covered his face with his hands.

His future seemed bleak. Now for his whole life, he would have to pretend to be the Brahmin son of a Brahmin father, knowing well in his heart that it was a lie; he did not really belong to the society he was in.

Dev shriveled at the thought. No; he could do all but that. If he continued to pretend like a noble-born Brahmin, he would be fooling himself, more than fooling the world; it would undermine his dignity; it would scatter his integrity. It was impossible for him to live a life of pretense. He could no more accept the special respect people offered to a noble Brahmin.

But, what else could he do? Should he tell the world he was a foster-child of his Brahmin parents? Should he go out in public to tell the world he didn't know who his father and mother were? Should he tell everybody he doesn't know which clan he was born in to?

In a society closely knit with the hierarchy of caste and class, he couldn't imagine of doing that either. He'd degrade himself in the eyes of people, if he did that. His self-esteem would not allow him to do that. He felt restless and frustrated at his strange predicament.

Under the night sky, Dev wandered, restless and lonely, shaken to the core of his being. His self-worth seemed to be at its lowest. His mind was clouded with thoughts and he felt completely at a loss. His physical body came from them to whom he was born. His mind belonged to them, who brought him up. To whom does he really belong? Is there a soul, as the Vedas declare? Is there an eternal identity of man that can never be tainted?

Dev was desperately searching for a way to get rid of the sinking feeling that the mere thought of his unknown birth was triggering within. Was there a way that would allow him to live with his head held high ever again?

Never in his twenty four years of life had he faced so much heartache. He was feeling lost and scared, and angry for no certain reason. He didn't know what to do with his anger and energy and the life that was left to him.

The darkness of the night gradually started to dissipate. Sitting on the branch of the champak tree, a lone Myna was chirping sweetly, heralding the beginning of a new day.

"Who am I, really?" Dev whispered to himself. His old self, the proud and accomplished young Brahmin scholar died yesterday. And the present Dev was merely a name allotted to a five feet eleven inches body that has no ancestry, no social identity.

Standing beneath a shady tree in the courtyard something was surging within his heart. At that moment Dev knew he had a calling.

Dev came out under the open sky and looked above. The sky was filled with a strange bluish light. Looking at it, his breath eased. He felt much comforted. The shelter of his known existence had been snatched away from him, but under the vast blue sky he felt the promise of a grander shelter. A deep sigh came out of his heart.

The morning breeze was caressing his cheeks. The horizon in the east was tinged with red. Dev felt an unknown grace descending upon him. It was calling him to explore his true identity in this universe. To answer this call would mean tearing him apart from his present existence. To answer this call would mean placing himself in the embrace of the scaring unknown.

Dev felt scared at the thought of abandoning the comfort and surety of his present life, however stagnant, disconsolate and futile it was for him now. A big sigh came out of his heart. Dev was in a dilemma.

However, something deep inside his heart kept telling him this calling was the harbinger of an amazing freedom and peace, not known to him so far. Dev breathed deeply in the fresh air of the dawn under the open sky, not knowing for certain which course of life he was going to follow.

Dev's restlessness grew as days passed. Apparently everything was same as before, but, his sense of not belonging to anybody, anything or any place made him distant, aloof and detached. A silent stir in his heart, behind his apparent calm, was eating him up from inside. His friends noticed him somber and withdrawn.

A restless longing kept haunting him day and night. Dev finally made up his mind. He resolved to abandon his home to follow his calling. He was determined to find his true identity in this universe — an identity that would allow him to live with his head held high; an identity that would again allow him to live a life of esteem.

It felt scary to embrace a life of uncertainty, though. But he had no other choice. Dev knew for sure that his mind would not allow him to belong to his present state of life as a village Brahmin, or as a teacher of the Vedas.

Only Brahmins had the right to teach the Vedas, the scriptures say. And he really was an outcaste. How can he pretend to be a Brahmin? Dev was feeling devastated and suffocated inside, to live a life of pretense.

He was uncertain about what he was going to do with the rest of his life. However, the one thing he was sure was that he would have to go far away from his present home and relations. Suddenly he remembered Sage Ramanam, who, people say, is the wisest man on the land. Dev must go to him and seek his guidance. If anybody could show him the way to anchor the lost ship of his life, it would be him.

Dev was feeling exhausted to recall his past. The strain of leaving home left him almost drained. He retraced his steps back from the window and came to the couch kept near the bed. Remembering the sad face of his mother tears came at the corner of his eyes as he reclined on the couch.

Leaving home was not easy. The tie of their love and affection was stronger than he thought, and he felt much pain when he left his parents to pursue his search.

On the night before the morning he decided to leave, Dev went to his mother. She was sitting on a small stool in her veranda. She was anxious to get him a chair. Dev restrained her. He tried to smile in an effort to lighten the atmosphere. However his heart was heavy with the pang of imminent separation.

"Ma, today your son has come to beg something from you." He said benignly.

Hema was feeling overwhelmed with affection for his son. She remembered the days when little Dev used to come to her requesting her to make a toffee treat for his friends.

"There is nothing in this world, Dear son, that your mother can't give you for your happiness," she said.

Dev lowered his head. "Then, please give me permission to go and study under the guidance of the Sage Ramanam."

Hema became still like a statue. Tears rolled down from her cheeks.

"But what's the need of this?" She said in a faint voice. "Do you want to leave us, Dev? Would you become a monk?"

"I don't know, Ma. I want to find my real identity as a human being on earth; as a soul in this vast universe." He said hesitantly. "I need your blessings for that."

"I knew I could not retain you for long." Hema wept. She kept her trembling hands on the head of her son. "Your mother's blessings will always be with you, Dev." She said in a voice choked with tears, "May God protect you and make you happy, my son."

A drop of tear appeared in his eyes too. Wiping it with the back of his hand, Dev hurriedly took leave from his mother and went to his father. The old man was reclining on his couch. Startled, he opened his eyes when Dev touched his feet and stood silently in front of him. He looked up with question in his eyes.

"I want to go to study under the guidance of Sage Ramanam." Dev said.

The old man was taken aback. "No!" He shook his head in disbelief. "You can't leave us like that, Dev."

Dev remained silent.

"Don't go away from us." His father tried to persuade him again. "Together we'll teach the students in our Gurukul. Your mother will find a noble-born bride for you and you'll settle down here, among the people you grew up with."

Dev was silent for a moment. He was sorry to see the old man pained and puzzled. "Please. Don't try to stop me. I need to do this. Give me your permission." He said softly.

"Why? Why must you go away, Dev?" The old man said feebly in faint resistance. However, he knew his son well. He admired him secretly for his inner strength, will and determination.

"Are you going forever?" He said again.

"I don't know." Dev said in low tone.

"When do you wish to leave?" The old man asked again.

"Tomorrow..."

"May you succeed in your endeavors, my Son," the old man said feebly; his voice trembled. A flood of affection for his old father surged in his heart; Dev restrained himself. He touched his feet again, and left.

Nobody slept in the house that night. Dev decided to leave at daybreak, without waking them up. Their tears and sadness was weakening him from inside. He left silently, when it was still dark and walked briskly toward the south. On the way he got a bullock cart going toward the capital

city Nandanar; it was carrying goods for trading. The
driver agreed to take him to the city and they left.

##

At dusk the cart reached a small hamlet on the roadside.
The lush green rice-fields extending toward the horizons
relaxed his eyes. A few small mud cottages and straw-
huts were seen around. The cart stopped in front of a
walled courtyard. There were three small huts within,
surrounded by a mud wall beneath a row of tall Eucalyptus
trees. On enquiry from the driver Dev knew that the name
of the village was Malia.
"We'll rest here tonight and resume our journey early in
the morning," said the driver. Dev had no other option but
abide by his wish. He jumped down from the cart to look
around.
A girl came out of the house in a moment — a pretty little
creature with round face and grayish blue eyes; her curly
brown hairs went down her slender back. Her face was
bright and full of enthusiasm. She looked at Dev curiously.
Dev let his eyes linger on the small form wondering if she
was malnourished. She was much too tiny in his eyes. He
tried to learn more from her appearance but he couldn't
see anything besides her beautiful curls and flawless skin.
The driver came forward and said, "Sania! How're you?
Where's your mother?"
So Sania is her name, he thought. The girl smiled. Her
white teeth sparkled between her full lips.

"Ravi uncle!" she said in a delightful voice, "Please come in; Mom's yet to return from the field; you know, the crop's ripe and there's lots of work in…"

She disappeared inside, without finishing her words. Dev and Rabi entered the yard. The girl came out from a hut with two low cane stools in her hands. She placed them on the yard in front of them.

She shot him a smile. Dev gave a slight smile and said "Namaste," joining his hands near his chest; he was feeling somewhat awkward, without anybody introducing him. She smiled again saying nothing and disappeared in one of those huts.

The driver was a jovial person. Dev couldn't guess his age. His seasoned brown face, sturdy appearance and gray hairline told he might well be anywhere from fifty to sixty. He offered Dev a stool to sit on, lighted a cigar made of Sal leaves as he sat on the other and started humming a folksong.

The girl came back with a jug full of water and two glasses. Dev was feeling very thirsty. He thanked the girl politely after he finished three glassful of water. She was staring at him with curiosity and amazement. As Dev's gaze met hers, she lowered her gaze. She was in her late teens, fair, slender and modestly dressed in a long pale blue skirt reaching her toes, pink blouse and a white scarf wrapped around her neck.

The girl went inside the hut again and Ravi kept murmuring his song. Dev was feeling very tired. The stress of leaving home made his mind somewhat blank, unresponsive and uninterested to the surroundings. He became lost in his thoughts. He was startled to hear a female voice from his back.

"Is it Ravi Dear? How're you?" It said. Dev turned around to find an old woman with a bundle of twigs on her head. Promptly he stood up to help her put it down. The woman looked at him with appreciation and admiration in her eyes.

"Thank you, Son; may you live long!" She said and blessed him. She had many wrinkles on her forehead, but had a beautiful smile. Dev made a bow to her and said "Namaste".

The driver, Ravi was his name, Dev knew by this time, came forward. "This gentleman is going to the capital city with me, Sister. He is from the village Mandira." He said, guessing her curiosity.

"Oh, I see," she said looking at him, respectfully.

Dev could not make out whether this woman was really Ravi's sister, or they were mere old acquaintances. After enquiring about Ravi's family and his business, the woman turned toward Dev.

"Sir, you seem to be a Brahmin. We are farmers. Will you take your meal from us?" She said in respectful anticipation. "Otherwise, I may manage to bring some food for you from the Shastris, the only Brahmin family in our village."

Dev felt a stir again within his heart and he tried to suppress it. What would he say? He himself didn't know what he really was. Even these poor villagers are fortunate in that they've got a lineage to belong to, while he has none. —

"My name is Dev." He said humbly. "Please call me by my name. I will be pleased and grateful to accept meal from you."

The woman was surprised and evidently pleased. She proceeded toward the hut. The young girl came out. "He already had water from me, Ma." She whispered.

"Sania"; her mother shot her a 'be quiet' look; "Will you stop your chatter and come to help me prepare the meal?"

Dev, not feeling at home, stood up and said, "I'd like to go out to see around the village, Ravi." Before the man could say anything, a voice came from inside the hut, "No, Son. It is already dark now. There are snakes in the paddy fields. Tomorrow morning Ravi will show you around."

The old woman came out from the hut with a portable mud stove and placed it on the patio in front of her hut.

"Tomorrow morning we'll be leaving. Won't we?" Dev said to Ravi. Ravi nodded to say 'yes'.

"What? Tomorrow morning?" The old woman said hurriedly, "No, no, Son, please stay with us a few more days." She pleaded, "The Holi festival is just around the corner. I think, you'll enjoy the festival in our village." Then turning to Ravi, she said, "And Ravi Dear, You hadn't been here for quite a long while. You must stay with us for a few more days this time."

Ravi looked up at Dev for his consent. The old woman sounded very earnest; it would be rude to turn down her request. But Dev hardly knew these people.

Before Dev could say anything, the woman said again, "We seldom have guests here. The whole village will be happy to host you, Son. Please don't put us down." Her words reminded him of how delightfully he used to celebrate Holi, the festival of colors, with his friends at Mandira. A sigh came out of his heart. Dev couldn't say anything.

Ravi evidently very happy at the proposal said, "Okay, Sister. I don't mind staying back for a few more days. What do you say, Sir?" He said turning to Dev, obviously expecting his consent.

Five days were left to the festival. Dev counted. What will he do here for so many days among these strangers? "Not so long. But we may stay back for a day or two."

"Okay, agreed." The old woman smiled. "Stay with us for a couple of days and if you don't enjoy your stay here we won't ask you to extend it up to the Holi."

Dev smilingly relented, though he was feeling impatient inside. He was sure he couldn't possibly enjoy anything at his present state of mind.

But the city is far away from here, at least three hundred miles, or even more, and no other conveyance is available except such goods-carrying bullock carts that occasionally pass by. Dev felt confounded.

Ravi seemed to be distantly related to this peasant family. He began to relate many fond memories of the olden days

when Sania's father was alive. With dry twigs, the woman
lit up the fire in her mud stove. Sitting on the floor by the
side of her mother, the girl was kneading the dough of
flour. Occasionally Ravi was chitchatting something
regarding his village friends and relations. The woman
busy in her cooking was replying briefly.

Dev was looking vacantly at the dark in the distant yard.
He didn't feel like listening to their conversations. There
was a vacuum in his head and he was trying, in vain, not to
remember his home in Mandira.

Absorbed in his thought, he was a bit startled as the girl
came up to him to announce that the food was ready. They
spread two cotton mats on the patio of the hut for them to
sit. The girl came with a brass pot in her hand and poured
water from it. After Dev and Ravi washed their hands and
faces, they sat down for the dinner. There were two brass
dishes and glasses in front of them that sparkled in the
mild light of the oil lamps. The food was simple,
cauliflower and potato curry, and Chapattis. Dev was
hungry. He ate with satisfaction.

After the dinner was over, Dev came out under the open
sky. The night sky was studded with stars. The fresh night
breeze was carrying the scent of an unknown flower. The
fragrance was intoxicating.

It brought back many childhood memories. Back home,
they had a bush of Night Queen in their courtyard. It
carried beautiful fragrant flowers in the night. The whole
yard would be fragrant with its wonderful scent. If little

Dev wanted to pluck the flowers from the bush, Hema won't let him do that. In the night fairies come to take flowers from the bush, she would tell him, taking him on her lap. "You would disturb them, Dear, if you touch the bush in the evening", she would say. The fond memories of his boyhood brought a smile on his lips.

Suddenly noticing a shadow beside him, he turned around. It was Sania. He didn't notice when she came. She came and stood there silently, amused to find him smiling, all alone by himself. Dev felt a little embarrassed.

"Your bed is ready, Sir". She said and smiled again. She led him to a hut at the farthest end of the courtyard. The hut was neat, but bereft of any luxury. Very cute white floral designs were painted on the floor and on the mud walls. These floral paintings, called Rangoli, are painted by rice milk. These wonderful works of art must be credited to this girl. He thought.

"You are an excellent artist, I see", Dev said, to strike up a conversation with the girl in an effort to come out of his embarrassment and uneasiness. The girl smiled. "You must be speaking of this Rangoli."

"Yes; I'm." Dev grinned.

"Every year on the day of the Holy festival, I clean the walls, wipe the paintings out with fresh mud, and draw them again with colored rice milk. They are auspicious, you know." She said, her face beaming with joy in the appreciation she just received.

"That's quite a job; isn't it?" he said.

"Yes, it is. Stay with us this Holi, and you will see the whole process yourself." She said.

Entering the hut, Dev found a wooden cot, with the bed neatly done on it. There was a quilt and a pillow on the clean bed sheet spread over the bed. A wooden cloth holder was hanging on the wall and a small brass-pot filled with water was kept on the small shelf carved on the wall. There was no other furniture in the room.

"Where is Ravi?" He enquired.

"He is staying in the hut beside ours. He stays there whenever he comes. He is a cousin of my mother." Sania said.

"I see," Dev said, relieved. He was badly in need of space and solitude. He was glad that he could sleep alone.

"This room remains empty most of the time, you know," Sania said, "except for the festival days when we have special worship performed by Pundit Ji."

The ordinary village folks typically address any and all priests and scholars as 'Pundit Ji'.

"Pundit Ji?"

"You don't know Pundit Ji?" Sania was shocked at his ignorance.

"No..." Dev nodded meekly, amused at her innocent presumption that he should know their village priest. "Who's he?" He asked presently in a sober voice, concealing his amusement.

"Everybody knows him in five villages surrounding ours." Sania proceeded to enlighten him in wide-eyed wonder.

"He is the village priest, the only one in the five neighboring villages! Very scholarly, very intelligent and educated in the Veda-mantras, he is the richest man in our village, you know." She said with obvious reverence in her voice and awe in her eyes.

Dev was amused at the naiveté of this simple village girl. Her innocent chatter was piercing through the gloom of his heart.

"Really!" he said, as he was noticing the expression of awe in her face.

"Yes!" said Sania, "He has a thick gray moustache and a long beard, like this!" she added, gesturing her hands to show the length of his moustache and beard. Dev was controlling his laughter with difficulty.

"He is a very serious type of person, you know; he always wears a look like he's been greatly disappointed for some reason," Sania said again, making faces to copy his facial expression.

Dev laughed aloud. Sania giggled too.

"Sania! Will you let him take rest?" The voice of her mother came from the cottage at a distance. Sania departed in a hurry with a reluctant look in her eyes.

Dev was feeling light at heart. This trifling talk with this simple village girl was removing his gloom. These people are amazing, he thought. Poverty couldn't daunt them down to rob them off their graceful tenderness. He laid his tired body down to the bed and drifted off to sleep almost immediately.

##

The golden Rays of the rising Sun touched his face as he woke up in the morning. Dev came out of his room to find nobody in the vicinity. He went for a stroll along the village road. The soil beneath his feet was coppery red in color. Tall, dense trees were standing on both sides, creating exquisite embroidery of shadow and light on the pathway.

Fresh morning breeze was mildly caressing his unkempt hair. He ran his hand through his wavy brown hair. Dev was feeling light at heart. He stopped to take a full breath. The air was fresh and fragrant with the scent of earth and greens.

Wide paddy fields were spread across miles after miles, as far as he could see. He stepped down the narrow pathway across the fields. He was walking without a purpose, without a destination. He suddenly had a feeling that told him he was the child of this universe. Earth was his home. Sky was his shelter. The whole of humankind was his family. He was feeling at ease with everything around him. It was such a sense of freedom.

But this feeling was very temporary. He knew. Behind his apparent calm, was lurking the feeling of restlessness and despair. A feeling of worthlessness was silently eating him up from inside. A deep sigh came out of the depth of his being.

Dev tried to forget the frustrating thoughts of his past. The fresh morning air was relaxing and soothing his being.

Presently he noticed a green creature on the road. It was a cute little grasshopper. He bent down to pick it up. The nice little creature rested for a while on his palm examining him with its round black eyes. Suddenly it jumped from his hands in to the paddy fields startling him and making him laugh.

"Why are you laughing alone?" A female voice said from his back. Astonished, Dev looked back to find Sania. She was walking his way.

"I wasn't alone, Sania." He said.

"How did you know my name?" She frowned. She was surprised and delighted at the same time.

"How did I know it? …I must have some occult power, you see!" He said, a smile of amusement still lingering on his face.

Sania tried to read through the expression on his face and nodded in disbelief.

"Ravi uncle must have told you." She concluded.

"No, Sania. Nobody told me. I have heard them calling you by this name."

"Oh!?" She changed the topic swiftly. "Now tell me why you were laughing alone."

"I wasn't alone, Sania; I told you." He said soberly.

"But you were alone. I have seen in my own eyes."

Dev suddenly became serious. His tone changed. "Our eyes, senses and even our minds don't always give us the correct information, Sania." He said.

Sania didn't seem to take note of what he said. She shrugged her shoulders in bewilderment. She was still looking at him with question in her wide eyes.

She won't understand what he meant to say, he thought with a sad smile. She was too busy with her everyday existence to bother with such lofty things.

"Okay. I'm telling you why I was laughing." Dev said running a hand through his wavy hair. "She was with me, you see." He casually pointed his fingers to the green creature sitting on a leaf in the field. "I was amused at her jumping around." He said again.

Sania glanced down and saw the little creature on the field. She broke in to a fit of laughter. "You are crazy!" she said giggling. Dev too joined her in the laughter.

Probably she had very little education, if any, as is common with these poor village women; still, with her merry spirit and liveliness, this pretty village girl was helping him to lift his spirit. Dev appreciated her simplicity, innocence and enthusiasm. He glanced above. The Sun was becoming warmer.

"I've been searching for you for quite a while. Let's go home." Sania said, "Mother has made rice pancakes for breakfast." Quickly they headed toward their hut.

The aroma of the food was spread around the little hut. As Dev entered the hut, he found them waiting for him. He felt ashamed to keep them waiting. Sania's mother served him with such care and respect that made Dev feel a bit uneasy.

The food was tasty. Ravi was sitting beside him, busy to do justice to his food. After a while, when his plate was empty, Ravi found respite to talk. While Sania was pouring tea in the cups, he said to her mother, "Sister, aren't you searching for a suitable boy for Sania? She is already twenty. It's about time you should have thought about getting her married with a suitable boy." Suddenly there was a somber silence in the atmosphere. Sania went inside the hut and her mother looked sad.

"You know, Ravi, how difficult it is for a poor widow like me to arrange for the marriage of my daughter." She said with a sigh. "Many proposals came. But I couldn't proceed; nor could they. You know how my finances are. How can a marriage be settled when you don't have money to feed the marriage party and adorn the bride with at least a silver chain and bangles?"

"Hmmm…" Ravi nodded anxiously.

"After feeding ourselves I have hardly any money left with me to save anything for her marriage." The old woman said sadly.

"I understand." Ravi nodded. "But we must do something, Sister. What will happen to her after you pass away?"

"I know Ravi." Sania's mother said with a sigh. "This worry is eating me up and I can't sleep well in the night."

There was a heavy silence for a while. "Something must be done about it." Ravi said. A furrow appeared on his forehead.

Dev was feeling very sad and somewhat uneasy, having been present there listening to their private conversation.

He had been brought up in luxury compared to this poor
peasant family. Back home they always had enough to eat,
enough to share and much to give away in charity. He had
no idea of the hardship, sorrow and suffering of the poor.

Sania's mother insisted him to take more pancakes.
Politely declining and excusing himself, he silently left the
place. The more he saw of this poor family, the more
astonished he became to find their incredible spirit of
grace, tenderness and hospitality.

Within a couple of days, his uneasiness and stiffness was
gone. Dev was feeling at home with these people. Sania
came to him whenever she got respite from her work and
chitchatted about this and that. She told funny village
stories, made faces while relating about the strange village
people she knew, and giggled. Dev stared at her in wonder
and amusement. He liked her company. The veil of his
sadness was slowly dissipating, and he felt much relieved.

##

Sania was cooking in the mud stove and Dev sat beside
her on a low cane stool. Her mother went to work in the
field. Rabi was out to visit some old friends. Dev noticed
Sania was wearing bangles made of colored glasses and
had a thick red thread around her neck, instead of a gold or
silver chain. He has always seen his mother wearing gold
bangles and jewelries.

He felt a bit uneasy remembering the fine gold chain
around his neck carrying a golden amulet in it. It was put

around him by his mother for his protection, since when he was a child.

"Are you a Brahmin?" She asked without turning to him.

"I don't know, Sania." He said in a low voice seeking to hide his desperation.

"You, educated people, always seem to speak in a riddle." She said and giggled.

"You must be very learned!" She said again.

"Why?" Dev could not but smile at her strange inference, which was correct, nevertheless.

"You didn't answer me." She frowned. "Have you gone to school?"

"School...? I had my own...!" Dev cut his sentence short realizing that he didn't wish to reveal his story. "Okay!" He said presently, snapping his fingers, "I've studied a little, Sania."

"I see;" she frowned again, "How much? Can you write letters?" She asked curiously.

"Yes!" He said smiling at her words. "I have studied a little of literature, grammar, history and also the Vedas."

"Good God!" Sania gasped and turned from the cooking stove with the spatula in her hand. "You know the Veda mantras!" She said in wide-eyed wonder and amazement. "Then you are a scholar like our Pundit Ji!"

The very fact that she seemed shocked by his answer brought a smile to his lips. In some ways, she was very cute. She was like a cute little puppy.

"But you are a better guy than him." She said again.

"How did you know?" He asked, amused.

"I know." She said thoughtfully, "He is very much conceited. His manners are not as good and gentle as yours. Besides, you accept meals from us, though we belong to a lower caste. It's so nice of you."

Dev smiled. A shadow of sadness spread around his eyes. He has always abhorred those stringent social rules of higher and lower castes. He felt amazed at how the study of the Vedas narrowed the visions of those Brahmins, instead of expanding it. They undermine the essential dignity of human being.

Sania did not seem to notice the change of mood in him. Her cooking was almost complete.

"After your lunch is over, I'll go to the field, you know." She said. "I'll take my lunch there with my Mother."

"Okay." Dev nodded. "What about Ravi?"

"Oh, I hope he will be back by the time I leave for the field. If he is not, then I'll put his food down right there inside his hut with a cover on it." She answered promptly. "You would sure like to accompany me to the field. Won't you?" She asked.

"Sure!" Dev smiled. In a way he was learning important lessons from this simple village girl. She knows to take on life on her own terms and she is thoroughly enjoying her life with its many struggles and adversities.

Sania was walking briskly in light steps among the narrow pathways across the paddy fields. She had a bundle of food, and water-pot on her head, supporting that in one hand. The other was hanging loosely by her side swinging in a rhythm as she walked on. In her violet Sari wrapped around her little frame she looked like a beautiful butterfly dancing down the lush green fields.

Dev was walking behind her. These easygoing, hardworking villagers and their simple lifestyle enchanted him much. He was increasingly amazed to find their incredible spirit. This type of carefree lifestyle was all very new to him.

He was also amazed to notice a change within him. Is happiness contagious? Dev wondered. Their simple happiness was penetrating his being, erasing his sadness and easing his mind with an unknown cheerfulness. He was worrying little about his past; nor was he concerned about what future has kept in store for him. Like these simple village folks he was floating in a pure joy of living in the moment. He was very happy with these people.

Sania's mother was working in their small field, her forehead glistening with sweat. She was very happy to see Dev. Sania sat down beneath a shady Banyan tree beside the field. She uncovered the food and two of them, mother and daughter, had their meal together on two large banana leaves.

Dev was strolling around the field. After they were finished with their meal, Sania waived her hands to call him. "Come here, Pundit ji! I'll show you around." She said.

Her mother shot her a warning look turning from her work. "Sania!" she screamed; "That's enough of your teasing." Sania became very sober. She lowered her head. Her mother went back to her work in the field.

Glancing over her shoulder, when she saw that her mother had her back turned to them, she giggled surreptitiously and bowed to Dev, joining her hands in a sham show of reverence. Dev glared at her, pretending anger.

They were walking together side by side amid the yellowish green pastures. Mostly Sania was continuing with her chatter about this and that. Dev was a patient listener. After a while they reached a field, an almost bare expanse, covered by sands. A narrow river was flowing across it. There was not a trace of any human habitation around. Only a line of faint bluish green mountains was visible on the horizon. This was probably the farthest end of the village.

"This is our river Kanka; there, from the mountains she comes." Sania said, as she sat down on a piece of rock. "Isn't our village beautiful?"

"Indeed, it is." He took a deep breath, admiring the landscape.

"You told us almost nothing about you and your village", she said. "Won't you tell us anything about yourself?" she said with a grin. "Where do you come from? Who is there in your family? Why are you going to the city?" She asked all in a breath.

Dev could not but smile at her way of questioning.

"Wait a minute." He said smiling, "You are running like a roller!"

Sania frowned at this. "Okay. Don't tell anything about you, if you don't like." Her voice sounded heavy.

"I don't have much to tell about me, Sania". Dev said, leaning against a rock that tilted over the river. "I came from the village Mandira, you know. I have nobody but my parents... my foster parents, at home."

"Oh! I see. You must have lost your parents at an early age..."Sania said, her voice tender with sympathy. She did not wait for a reply.

"Didn't you marry?" She asked again.

"No...;" he grinned.—

Not this topic again! He moaned inwardly.

"Why?" She asked presently in innocent wonder.

Dev laughed aloud. "Sania, let's go home. It's getting dark. Your mother will be worried." He said, wishing to divert her from the topic. Sania was not the one to be so easily distracted. She stood up unwillingly, but did not move. Walking a few steps forward Dev turned around, startled that she wasn't right with him.

She waited for him to come back.

"What happened? Sania, come on!" He said, puzzled. They started walking back toward their hut.

"You didn't tell me why you didn't marry." She said again.

Dev was silent for a while. He didn't know why such a trivial thing should bother her.

"Ah...There were important things I was doing, Sania, and... I didn't think it was time to settle down, you know." He rambled.

Sania had a surprised look in her eyes.

"Really?" She said, turning toward him, "But in our village most of the boys of your age are married and settled with their own family and children, you know."

"I see; and what about the girls?" He asked casually.

"The girls are married much earlier." She said solemnly. "All my friends are married. A few of them live here in our village, and some are settled in the neighboring villages."

Her head dropped down. She knew her mother was too poor to pay for her wedding.

Dev was pained to see her in a somber mood. "I…I didn't mean to hurt you," He said contritely, "I'm sorry, Sania, if I did." Sania was unusually silent the whole way they walked back to their hut.

##

Only a couple of days were left to the Holi festival, the festival of colors. Sania's mother was busy preparing sweets for the occasion. Every household in the village was preparing for the special festival of colors. Women from the neighboring huts kept coming and going. Some brought specially prepared sweets for their guest. Some stared curiously at him, inquisitive to know the whereabouts of this handsome stranger with a regal air. Dev was feeling ill at ease at their curiosity. Mostly he kept himself confined in his room, except for the mealtime.

Sania came to his room and chattered about this and that, whenever she took a break from her household chores. Dev was sometimes amused, sometimes curious or surprised to hear her recount many incidents of their humble life.

In the morning of the day before the Holi festival, she peeped in to his room as he just woke up. She cleaned and wiped the room, the floor and the walls thoroughly. It took her the whole day to clean and wipe up their huts with mud-water. In the afternoon, she grinded some rice that she soaked in water from the previous night. In this dense rice milk, she mixed some gum of a tree.

"This is to make it stick on the walls, you know", she said to enlighten Dev, as her hands were busy preparing the mix. She prepared several such mixtures of various colors in different bowls, mixing turmeric paste for yellow, vermillion for red, powdered indigo leaf for blue and a special kind of clay to make a saffron mix. Dev was a charmed observer of her artistry. He was observing her, sitting silently beside her on a cane stool.

By the evening she finished drawing beautiful floral designs of many colors on the floors and walls of the huts. After she finished drawing the last line, she looked up at him and smiled.

"How do you like it?" She asked in a casual voice, hiding her excitement.

"They are superb, excellent....fantastic!" He said in sincere applause. She blushed at his appreciation. "I've never seen in my whole life such an excellent Rangoli," he said again; "You need to be rewarded for this."

"Nobody had ever praised me like you did; thank you", she said. She was beaming in joy. Suddenly she lowered her voice and added, "I never had a friend like you, you know." She said with a graceful glance before disappearing through the door.

Dev was startled to hear this. He smiled silently. He didn't know from when in this short stay he too started to feel a strange bond of affection with this peasant family. But now is the time to leave, he felt, before this bond grows stronger, before they become too attached to him. 'Now, or never!' Something whispered within him. He felt a weird unrest within. A strange sadness crept in to his heart.

Late in the night, after the dinner, Dev came out of his cottage. Moonlight flooded the terrace. He found the mother and daughter sitting quietly on their veranda. The whole village seemed to be asleep under the full moon.

Seeing Dev walking their way, her mother bade her to enquire if he needed anything. Dev took a cane tool to sit near them and said, "Please don't worry about me. You and your daughter have taken care of everything I might have needed."

Sania's mother smiled. "Even in this short time, you have been so close to our hearts, Son... it seems you'd never been a stranger to us." She said.

Dev smiled too. "I'm feeling the same, you know... so much so that I feel really sorry that it's time to leave."

"Leave? When?" The old woman was taken aback. Sania was startled beyond limit, but she kept quiet.

"The day after tomorrow." Dev said softly. He noticed in the moonlight Sania's face turning pale.

"You should have stayed a few more days with us, Son." The old woman pleaded. "What's the hurry?"

"I wished I could stay a few more days." Dev said in an apologetic tone. "But, I have left my home with a purpose, you know... I can't rest till I accomplish my mission."

Dev was sure his words weren't making any sense to them. The mother and daughter kept silent. There was sadness in their eyes. Dev was feeling very sorry for them. He too felt that he knew them forever.

"I'll never forget your hospitality, care and affection," he said again. "You have been so nice and kind to me. I have a request to you before I leave."

The old woman looked at him with silent question in her eyes.

Dev took out the golden chain and amulet from his neck and held it out toward the old lady. "I beg you to keep this, Mother. I don't know how much it will be worth; but it surely will be enough to pay for the expense of her wedding."

At this moment Sania stood up and walked away to disappear in the room. The old lady was surprised beyond limit. She was evidently happy, though she denied accepting the gift.

"No, Son", she vehemently shook her head, "You were our guest. It was our pleasure to serve you. I can't accept any gift in return."

"Nothing can be worth the affection you two showered on me, Mother." Dev said earnestly. "This gift is only a small token of my respectful gratitude. Please accept it."

"I see an amulet with it. It must have been given to you for your protection." She said. "How can I take it?"

"It's not of any use to me. There'll be none happier than me if it comes to your use."

The old woman kept quiet.

"Please allow me to do this for you. I'll be more than happy if Sania is happily married in a good family." Dev pleaded again, persuading the old lady to accept the gold chain.

##

The morning came with colors. There was color, color and color everywhere. Dev stepped out of his room to find children, young men and women playing with colored water. They were playfully throwing colors to each other. They threw some colors to tinge his white shirt to red. As he walked out he found everywhere adults and children alike, singing, dancing and throwing powdered colors to each others. Even strangers threw colors to him and he smiled back.

But where was Sania? Dev did not find her anywhere. She was not in her room. She didn't come when he had his breakfast or lunch either. Dev looked for her in every place he knew, but could not find her. He hesitated to ask her mother, but when she did not turn up till the afternoon, he could not contain his worry. He approached the old lady sitting on the patio of her hut.

"I didn't see Sania today. Was she out to visit her friends?" He asked hesitantly.

"No, Son. I was searching her from the morning." Sania's mother said, "She didn't have her lunch either. Just a few moments back, I spotted her sitting beside the lake."

No sooner than her mother said this, Sania entered the terrace. Without saying a word to anybody she went to her room.

"Here she comes," her mother said with an affectionate smile, "Crazy girl! I'm sorry, Son for her poor manners."

Dev didn't know what to say. Ravi came back from the village colored from head to toe. He asked Dev if he would like to leave early in the next morning before the Sun rises high. Dev nodded at this and Ravi left to change his dress. Dev was noticing a sudden change in Ravi's gesture toward him. Ravi seemed to be all the more respectful and obliged to fulfill his wishes. Perhaps Sania's mother told him of his gift.

In the evening, women from the neighboring huts came. They distributed sweets to each others. But Sania did not come out of her room, even for once. She stayed inside her hut, with the excuse of having a headache. She didn't come out even to help her mother prepare the dinner. The poor old lady kneaded the dough and cooked alone to make chapatti and curry for the evening meal.

Dev was feeling very sad for Sania. She'd been so nice and kind to him all through. She is such a wonderful girl. He could not imagine that the news of his leaving would have such an impact on her. She did not come out even when he had his dinner. After the dinner was over, Ravi retired in his room. Sania didn't take any food the whole day. Nor did her mother take anything in the evening. Dev was feeling very sad for them. He approached Sania's mother. The old lady was busy packing food for them to take away in the morning.

"You didn't take any food, mother; neither Sania did." He said in a soft voice.

Her mother shook her head. "She's like that, Son. How much I pleaded with her; but she won't."

"I want to see her, before I leave tomorrow."

"She is awake, just pretending to sleep. Go there inside the hut, Son." She said.

Hesitating a little, Dev entered her room. He found Sania reclining on her bed with a blanket on her that covered up her whole body, even her face. With a slight hesitation, he knocked on the door and called, "Sania!" At this she removed the blanket from her face, and looked at him. In the dim light of the oil lamp her face looked red and her eyes too seemed to take on a reddish hue. Dev went inside and sat down at the corner of her bed.

"Are you angry with me, Sania?" he said in a low apologetic tone, "Please forgive me if I have committed any mistake without my knowing."

At this she sat up on the bed and wept.

"Sania, are you alright?" he asked. She covered her pale face with her hands and sobbed brokenly into them.

Dev was feeling dejected. He hated to see a lady in distress. However, he let her weep silently for a while, not knowing how to console her. After a while she seemed to regain her composure. Wiping her eyes with the back of her hands, she said, "What's the hurry? Why are you leaving us so soon?"

Dev was silent. He didn't know what to say. She came nearer to him. His body warmed from their close proximity. Dev was feeling a bit uneasy. Never in his life had he been in such nearness to a young woman. In the dim light of the room, with her red face, reddish eyes and disheveled hair, she looked prettier. Part of him couldn't believe what was happening. It almost seemed like a dream.

Sania suddenly flung her hands around his shoulders and whispered, "Dev, can't you stay with us forever?" She came closer so that they were almost touching.

"W-What do you mean, Sania?"

"Well, you never did answer my question."

"You know, I didn't come here to stay forever."

"I know that. But things are different now."

"I don't understand."

"You do understand, Dev; only you pretend not to understand. You know what I mean. Am I not pretty?"

Dev was clueless about what to say. "You are, Sania. You are one of the prettiest girls I have seen. But that doesn't make any difference to my mission."

"Your mission...? What mission?" Sania frowned. Dev kept quiet. He was searching for words to explain to her his strange predicament that made him abandon his home and vocation.

"I'll never be an obstacle to your mission. I love you, Dev", she said, and then in a bold move that even surprised her for she would never do such a thing with any man on earth, she closed the gap between them and kissed him on his cheek.

Dev was shocked beyond limit. His face grew red. He never knew when their innocent friendship changed its hue and the girl started loving him so desperately. Dev instinctively felt the urge to return her hug, but he resisted himself. She was looking very passionate. His hug could send the wrong message to her and the situation may go out of control. Dev was feeling very sorry for her. He was also feeling very helpless. He didn't know how to console her.

She felt his shock before he relaxed, took a deep breath, and gently patted her on her back. She knew what she had just done was somewhat unladylike; still she could not help her doing that. She felt so much attracted to this man from the very first day she met him.

His sculpted face and well-toned body could have been cut from marble for display in a temple. On the top of that he is so refined, cultured, dignified, generous, and chivalrous. Never in her life had she seen a more graceful young man. She could do anything to get him love her. But somehow she had always felt that he was so passionless; kind and gentle, but so high and saintly, and much above her world.

Sania pulled herself back and asked, "Why are you silent, Dev? Say something. I'll not keep you from going to fulfill your mission, whatever that may be. Can't you marry me before you go?"

Dev lowered his gaze and shook his head in desperation. "I can't Sania. That would be an irresponsible thing to do. I don't know where life is going to take me. I may never come back again."

Sania silently stared at him. She was morose.

"I am sorry, Sania; but I don't have a ground beneath me. How can I entangle your life with mine?" Dev said in a diffident tone, "I don't know whether I'll be successful in my purpose. I don't know whether I'll ever go back to my parents either. I don't know for certain what I'm going to do with the rest of my life..." He said, helplessness written on his face.

He paused for a while and sighed. Sania was staring silently at the dear face that she has come to adore so deeply, without herself knowing it.

"I told you the other day that I was the foster child of my present parents." He said again, "You know what? I didn't know that myself a few days ago. I don't know if you'll be able to understand the suffering I'm going through, since I knew that the 'Brahmin' identity, which I grew up with, was a false identity; since I knew that the identity and whereabouts of my real parents is unknown." He sighed.

Sania was feeling sorry for him. She could understand his restlessness. A heavy breath came out of her heart.

"My feeling of self-worth has been at its lowest ever since." He said again. "I still couldn't come in terms with this strange reality that destiny had kept in store for me, you know." He paused.

"I left my home and vocation to find my real identity and can't rest till I do that, Sania. The sweet shelter of a happy home is not for me now; such a state of mental anguish won't allow me to rest."

Sania was listening to him patiently. She could see frustration written on his face. "Go, if you must;" she said faintly, "but why did you have to give your chain away to pay for my marriage? Does it amend anything?"

"No Sania, it surely doesn't amend anything. Only, I consider it a privilege to do this for you. It was a gift from a dear friend who, though going far away, will never forget you." He whispered in an ardent tone. "Gold and silver has no value, Sania, compared to what I've got from you."

Sania took her gaze away from him and looked afar through the window. Her eyes again became filled with tears. Dev's heart was heavy at her distress.

"Please! Sania, don't take it otherwise." Dev said keenly taking her hand in his, "I value your friendship more than anything on earth."

Sania stared back on him silently with tears sparkling in her eyes.

"The course of my life is uncertain, you know. I want you to be happily married and settled in your life." Dev said again with a deep sigh.

"I'm not keen to marry; why are you so keen about my marriage?" She said diffidently.

"Because, I'm your friend and I'm concerned about your wellbeing." Dev said softly. "Don't be obstinate, Sania. Your mother is growing old. How happy she will be to see you settled in your life before she breathes her last!" He said again.

"Where will you go?" She asked, taking her gaze back again to the window.

"I am not sure, Sania, where my search will take me away. Presently I'm going to the capital city Nandanar. I wish to study to sage Ramanam." He said.

"You've been very nice and kind to us. Thank you." She said, glancing at him, smiling faintly.

"No, Sania," Dev nodded desperately. "Please don't say so; it was not kindness." He said. "Everything I did was a gesture of gratitude. I'll ever cherish your friendship in my heart for my whole life. I've learnt a lot from you, Sania. It's you who has unknowingly taught me the secret of happily taking on life as it comes every moment."

Her eyes became filled with tears again. Both of them sat silently. The night breeze rustled through the window breaking the deep silence of the hour.

After a while, she wiped her tears away and said, "Okay; I accept your gift. Take good care of yourself. May God fulfill your mission, my friend." She smiled trying hard to cover her sadness.

"Now I'm feeling hungry." She said again, "Would you like to have a share of my meal? It's long while till you had had your dinner."

"Sure," he said smiling, "but just a little, if you wish so; you haven't taken anything the whole day." He paused a little and said "You are amazing, Sania. Thank you, thank you for everything..."

They came out on the veranda. Sania's mother was sitting there, reclining on the wall, her head drooping on her shoulder as she dozed. Dev felt sorry for the old lady. Sania woke her up. Three of them shared the meal among them and they ate in silence.

Early in the morning, Dev woke up to find the carriage ready for them to depart. When he was ready, he saw Sania and her mother standing on their courtyard in tearful eyes. Dev went near them. "Thank you for everything, Sania;" he whispered to Sania, his voice choked with emotion; "I'll never forget your friendship." Sania blinked back her tears.

"And thank you, mother; take good care of yourself." He said to the old woman and hurried out of the place. It wasn't until he made it to his carriage that he allowed himself to take a deep breath and exhale. He could see the old woman and her daughter waving their hands as the carriage left for Nandanar. Dev's heart became heavy.

##

Dev left the couch to go to the window again. He was feeling very restless. Life is so strange, he thought. Everywhere, on every land, you find friends and dear ones, when you are ready to open your heart. Love is such a strong bond. Is it more powerful than the bond of blood? He wondered. He was looking far away through the window, completely absorbed and lost in his thoughts. Hearing a mild knock on the door, he turned around. He found Jivan standing there. "Sir, please come to the dining hall. The meal is ready," he said.

A Solitary Flower with No Roots

Dev found Shyam waiting for him in the dining room. He greeted him with a cordial smile. A middle-aged man was standing there in the dress of the cook. He started serving the food, after they were seated. The food was simple, healthy and nutritious. Dev was hungry. He ate without a word. Shyam insisted him to take more. He'd been kind and affectionate toward him, without a reason; Dev thought with silent gratitude.

After they finished, a servant came with a tray with a silver teapot and cups on it. Placing the tray on the table, he went away at the bidding of Shyam. Shyam took the tray near him. He was pouring the tea.

"You didn't tell, my friend, where you came from." He said. "Would you mind telling me more about your village and your family?"

Dev looked up to him and paused for a moment unsure about what to say. "I came from the village Mandira." He said with some hesitation.

Mandira is a small, prosperous village at the border of the Kingdom, mostly inhabited by the learned Brahmins. Shyam heard about the place before, though he'd never been there.

"I see," he said, "you must have come from a Brahmin family."

Dev kept quiet for a moment; he felt that inner turbulence again. Though he came from a Brahmin family, in truth, he wasn't one of them. His true identity was unknown to him. He took a deep breath to hide his desperation.

"Yes Sir, but please excuse me if I can't tell you any further." He said humbly, "Because I myself don't know all the answers."

Shyam was taken aback. "What do you mean? Are you alright?"

"I mean exactly what I said, Sir. I know very little about myself." He said on a sad note. "Dev is just a name, a solitary flower with no root." He sighed, lowered his sad eyes and was lost in his thoughts.

Shyam was surprised at his somber reaction, but he was adept in concealing his feelings. He was a level-headed person, who didn't lose his cool easily. In his first impression the boy sounded arrogant; but on an afterthought, he changed his opinion. There must have been some deep hurt within this boy, he thought. — If he doesn't want to tell anything about himself now, it's okay.

Shyam was sure that his assessment about the boy couldn't go wrong. Never in his life had he gone wrong in reading human character. He'd seen noble aspirations in his eyes and there isn't enough reason to alter his judgment about the boy.—

"More milk for your tea, Dev? Shyam asked, holding the shiny silver pitcher aloft.

"No thank you, Sir," Dev said, "I'd prefer a little more sugar in mine."

"Sure!" Shyam passed the cute crystal sugar bowl. Both of them sipped the tea in silence.

"Take rest for now; we'll talk later, Dev. I am sorry, if I've hurt you, unknowingly." Shyam said, just before they departed after the lunch.

Dev didn't know how to respond to this kindness. Silent tears of gratitude welled up in his heart. He tried to smile.

"Thank you for your kindness and understanding, Sir." He said benignly, "Destiny has weaved a strange story around me, you know…"

Shyam was in a hurry to leave for the court. He mildly patted Dev on his shoulder and said, "You have come a long way, young man. Take rest. We'll meet again in the evening."

Dev returned to his room. He felt really tired. Sleep overtook him, as soon as he reclined on the pillow.

The Fortune Teller

In the morning, the royal court is usually filled with the visitors, petitioner and traders. Some come to ask for a favor, some for justice. Many come in the hope of selling something precious to the King, in lieu of a good price. This morning the court was almost empty.

King Vikram, his ministers and other high-ranking officials were discussing among them a proposal for the distribution of water of the Ganges with the neighboring Kingdom. A guard came to announce that a fortune-teller is waiting at the gate begging the audience of the King. Shyam stared at the King, trying to guess his mood. The former smilingly nodded his approval.

The gatekeeper entered with an old man. His hairs were white as the Kash flowers that blossom in the autumn filling the field and the riverside with their white splendor. Shyam was observing him keenly. The man folded his hands to make a bow to the King. He was perhaps in his eighties, tall and thin, having a burnt brown color. His eyes were clear and bright, unusual to one of his age. He was offered a chair.

He was panting and perspiring. Shyam ordered an attendant to bring a glass of water for him. The man made him seated, drank the water and blessed the King and the court.

"Your Majesty, I've come here to tell you something important, if I've permission to say."

"Tell his Majesty whatever you want to." Shyam said.

The man began to cough. "I've known that within a few years, our country is going to have an exceptional young King." He said, recovering. "By the virtue of his enlightened intelligence, wisdom, valor and merit, he will surpass all the previous ones that had graced the throne of our country." The old man paused.

The King and all the courtiers frowned at his words. A grave silence fell on all.

Adi, a senior minister cleared his throat. "We do not have a Prince, you know." He said. "Our King has a daughter, his only daughter. Do you mean to say that in a few years, our country would be invaded by a foreign ruler?"

"No, Sir. You've got me wrong. The King that is going to grace the throne would come from our own land."

"Really?" Prime Minister Shyam frowned. He was trying to guess, whether this old man was serious or was he cooking up a story.

"Yes Sir!" The fortune-teller went on, "By his virtue and prowess, he would conquer the heart of all." The man paused for a moment. "He will also conquer the heart of our Princess," he added with a smile.

A sigh of happy relief was spread in the court. The King was happy to hear the possibility of his daughter liking an able person who could be the heir apparent to the throne.

"Would he belong to a noble family?" asked the King.

"Yes, Your Majesty; but he will be like a tree of rare species". —

Nobody could make any sense out of these words. However, the King was happy. He ordered the royal treasurer to reward this man with ample gold coins, and dismissed him.

Lila and Bella were sitting in the Palace garden. A Palace-maid came running to announce that a fortune-teller came in the royal court.

Lila took it light-heartedly. "Surely, he cooked up a good story! Didn't he?" she asked in a light spirit.

"He was telling about the future King, My Princess!" There was excitement in the voice of Mitra, the Palace maid.

"Really?" Lila frowned; "and where will you get the future King? Is someone going to invade us?"

"No, my Princess. God forbid that." The maid said cutting her tongue. "Our future King will conquer the heart of the people of this land. He'll also conquer the heart of our Princess, the fortune-teller says." She ended with a smile.

Lila was flushed at her comment. Before she could say something, Bella intervened.

"This is good news Mitra." She said, taking the chain from her neck and giving it to her. "You deserve your reward for carrying this good news." The maid was overjoyed to receive the unexpected reward. She took the chain, bowed to the Princess and her friend and went off.

Lila frowned at Bella. "What is this Bella?" She reproached, "When did you start believing in these charlatans, who claim to know the future?"

Bella smiled meekly at the impatience of her friend. "You never know, my friend. There may be truth in his words." She said in her defense, "Why? Not all of them are frauds. This one may be genuine…"

"And why did you give away your chain to her?"

"I gave my chain to Mitra, because her story gladdened my heart; because her story said, somebody is going to win the heart of my dear friend!"

"You are crazy!" said Lila, smiling.

Who Am I?

On the dining table, two of them ate in silence. Shyam was a man of few words and he was hesitant to ask Dev anything lest he remind him of some painful memory. This boy had something within him that made him like him from the beginning. This was strange.

"Sir, when are we leaving tomorrow?" Dev said, breaking the silence.

"We'll leave early in the morning, Dev", said Shyam, "It will take us a couple of hours to reach the foot of the mountain, if we take a horse carriage, and we'll return before the Sun is too hot."

Dev looked up. "Yes Sir, but you certainly meant to say that you'll come back, leaving me there." He said.

"Obviously," Shyam said. But he was thinking something else. He was inwardly wondering at his strange feeling of affection to this young boy even within such a short time. For a seasoned statesman like him, this was something unnatural. Logic and rationality had always guided his intellect before. Now, he started thinking about means to keep this boy from going. What was happening to him? Is he interested to keep him just because of the many noble qualities he possesses? He argued within himself. No, that certainly doesn't explain why he was unwilling to let him go. He dismissed his own argument. However, presently he found a good excuse to keep him from going.

"But I was thinking something else, Dev." Shyam said in a serious tone. "The Sage leaves in a narrow cave on the mountain, you know. There is hardly enough space to accommodate another person. Where'll you stay there?"

Dev was puzzled, but he was determined in his purpose. "Sir, perhaps I'll find another cave for myself?" he said.

"Don't be crazy, Dev. That's next to impossible."

"But I'm determined to go and study with him, Sir; I'll definitely find a way."

"Sure you will, but not now." Shyam said with authority in his voice, "If you go and stay with him now, that would create inconvenience for both of you".

"Then what do you suggest me to do, Sir?"

"I'd advise you to stay back here for a few more days. By the time, I'll arrange to build a small cottage for you near the cave of the saint, with his permission. Until the cottage is built, visit the saint from my place whenever you like, and I'll be pleased to accompany you sometimes, whenever I'll find respite from my royal duties."

Shyam's advice sounded logical and practical. Dev decided to give in to this proposal.

"That sounds perfect. I'm really grateful to you, Sir, for your kindness." He said, inwardly wondering about his fortune. However he became very grateful to this man for his benevolence toward him.

The following morning at daybreak a horse carriage was ready to take them to the mountains. It took them about a couple of hours to reach the foot of the mountain where the sage lived. Dev was fascinated by the sight of the verdant mountain standing tall in the mid of the lush green valley.

Alighting from the carriage they began to climb the mountain through the small grassy mountain pathway. The path was not very steep. It was covered with dry leaves, twigs and flowers. They found tall trees and shrubs standing on both sides. Creepers laden with flowers of vibrant red, yellow and violet were hanging from above on the branches of the trees.

Along the slopes of the mountain there was a dark forest of rose-oaks and fir groves. Dev was enchanted by the breathtaking sight of the snowy mountain range at a distance and the green valley below.

Presently he noticed his companion having difficulty to keep pace with him. Shyam was short of his breath as he tried to keep pace with him. Dev felt ashamed. How could he be so self-centered and so immersed in himself? He didn't take notice of the difficulty of this elderly friend. Dev stopped to give his hand to help him. Shyam smiled in appreciation. Dev suggested him to rest for a while and found a broad mossy stone beside the path to sit on.

They resumed the journey after a while. They had climbed up some three hundred feet now. They found Rhododendron trees all around them. Within half an hour, they reached the cave of the sage.

In front of the cave, there was a large expanse covered with tender green grasses. A beautiful green lake was seen at a distance. "The locals called it 'Rani Talao', the queen of the lakes, you know," Shyam said.

"It's really beautiful." Dev walked up to the lake. It was a natural lake high above the Himalaya, made of natural rainwater. The reflection of the tall trees around and the moss growing in its bottom made the water look like dark green emerald.

He found flocks of small fishes playing in it.

Shyam brought pieces of bread and biscuits with him. When he dropped the breads in the water, they came in thousands to feast on that. They were so fearless that they didn't go away when Dev tried to touch them in the water. They played and passed between his fingers. He was fascinated.

The sage was sitting on a mat in front of his cave. Shyam went near him and announced his presence uttering 'Om', the word of words. The sage turned back. He greeted them with a smile and a soft utterance of the same mantra. Shyam offered some sweets and fruits he brought for the saint. He joined his hands to make a bow and touched his feet, as was the custom to greet the holy men.

Dev followed his friend. He touched the feet of the sage and sat at a distance. The sage grinned at him. "So you've come!" he said, staring at him. "I was waiting for you." Dev was startled to hear this.

Shyam was surprised too. "Do you know him, your holiness?" he asked.

The sage nodded, moving his head both sides, and said, "No." The sage didn't take his eyes away from Dev. Dev was feeling a bit uneasy at the way the sage was staring at him.

"Who are you?" The sage asked him after a while.

People rightly say that the old man is a little crazy. He pondered within. However, Dev could see the calm contentment, peace and rays of wisdom in his silent eyes.

"Just now you told me, Sir, you were waiting for me to come to you." Dev said humbly. "I've come to you to find the answer to the question you just asked me, Sir. Who am I?"

He was looking straight at the eyes of the old man. His heart was telling him this was the man he needed to come to, if he wanted to resolve the riddle of his existence.

There was a silence. The sage did not take his eyes off his countenance. Dev was feeling a strange peace flowing from those silent eyes down to him, penetrating his being.

"Come and stay here. You'll find the answer yourself." The sage said.

Shyam couldn't quite make out anything of their conversation. Every bit of their conversation seemed a piece of puzzle to him; however, he kept quiet. Before departing, he told the sage that if he permits, he would make a hut built for Dev near his cave. The sage consented. They left after making prostration to the sage.

The Flute Player

Early in the morning every day Dev liked to go to the river. He would meditate there on the riverbank for hours. Ganges was not far from Shyam's house and it took him hardly fifteen minutes to reach there. This morning while he was meditating, a fine music reached his ears. He opened his eyes to locate the source. Looking around, he spotted a young lad of about twelve or thirteen, sitting at the farthest stair on the riverbank. He was playing raga Bhairavi, a morning tune on his flute. Dev was moved. He closed his eyes again and listened to the music with rapt attention.

The music made him remember his village. He could see himself walking leisurely with his friends and playing his flute beside the small brook near the forest at the end of the village. With this scene, came back all the memories of his home, his parents and his happy days in Mandira. Dev could see his mother igniting an oil lamp in the evening, placing it beneath the bush of holy basil in the courtyard, and him playing his flute beneath the night sky.

Dev learnt the art of playing the flute from a friend in his teacher's house. He had the divine gift of quickly mastering anything he put his hands on. Coming back to Mandira, Dev went to Sharan, the master flute player in the village to learn from him more about the Ragas.

Shraran taught him the subtle nuances of the Ragas that appropriately portrayed different moods of the day, season and human mind. Before long he could effortlessly play each of the Ragas to its perfection. Playing the flute became his passion.—

Dev's heart ached as he was reliving those memories. He opened his eyes to distract himself. His glance met with that of the flute-player. He smiled and the boy smiled back. The boy finished playing his music and was about to leave. Dev requested him to sit near him for a while.

"You play very nicely, brother," he said.

"Thank you," said the boy.

"Where did you learn to play the flute?"

"From my dad. He is a musician in the royal court, you know." Pride for his father was evident in his voice.

"Oh, really!" Dev said. "My name is Dev. I'm very glad to meet you."

"I am Lalit," said the boy. "Do you come here often?"

Dev smilingly nodded in affirmation.

"There's our house," the boy said, pointing to a medium sized cottage at a distance and smiled. "Okay. Let me go today. We'll meet again."

The boy ran toward their cottage and Dev got up from his seat. He made him remember the companion of his olden days, the only one left now; his flute. Dev didn't play his flute since the bizarre evening his father recounted to him the strange story of his life.

##

The King and his friend were relaxing in the Palace garden having a casual chat in the evening. A sweet music of flute came floating in the air. They stopped talking to listen to it. The music was rich and melodious, a tune perfectly matching the mood of the evening. Like a mountain stream gliding through the stones, the melody was rising and falling in its effortless glide from one note to another. They became very silent allowing them to be soothed by its cadence. The music was, as if, sweeping the valley in its flow. It slowly faded away and disappeared. The King was enthralled.

"Who's this wonderful flute-player?" he asked, "I think the music was coming from your house, Shyam!"

The music surely was coming from his house. But Shyam had no clue about who the flute player was. Could it be Dev? Sure, it was him; who else could it be? This boy turns out to be exceptionally gifted! Presently he found the King staring at him, waiting for his reply.

"Yes, my friend." He said hesitantly, "It was Dev, perhaps."

Looking at the puzzled face of his friend, Shyam realized that his reply was incomplete.

"I found this boy meditating on the bank of the Ganges, you know." He said again. "He said he came from the village Mandira, wishing to study with Sage Ramanam."

"Hmmm! Sounds interesting!" The King said raising his eyebrow.

Shyam felt somewhat embarrassed. "The boy comes from an erudite Brahmin family, I think." He added somewhat hesitantly. "He is dignified and gracious. I invited him to stay as my guest."

"Hmmm!" The King was inquisitive. Shyam is wise, prudent and has good judgment of human character. The very fact that he liked the boy and invited him to stay in his house says much about the boy. And sure he is talented; this heavenly piece of music is the proof.

"Won't you introduce your guest to me, Shyam?" The King said.

"Sure! I will." Shyam said. "I'll bring him tomorrow afternoon." But there was hesitation in his mind thinking about Dev's reservation about discussing about his family.

"May I request you something, my friend?" He said again with some hesitation.

"Oh, come on! What's this Shyam!" The King said impatiently. "You don't need to be so formal with me."

"I know," Shyam smiled. "Please don't ask the boy about his family; he's probably got some hurt from his family and still couldn't get over it."

"Okay, my friend," The King nodded his consent. "So be it!" he said, inwardly smiling at his friend's sensitivity toward the boy. "But please request him to bring his flute."

Shyam smilingly nodded his approval and took leave.

##

Dinner was served in the evening. Shyam was looking curiously at Dev over the dining table. He was gracious, polite, and introvert as usual.

"Was it you, Dev," Shyam asked, "who played the flute in the evening?"

"Yes, Sir." Dev smilingly nodded.

"It was wonderful!" Shyam was enthused. "I didn't know you played flute so well. The King is enchanted with your music, you know."

"It is the companion of my childhood, you know." He said, "I learnt it from a friend in my Gurukul."

"But, you play like an expert, Dev; and there is more to it than simple expertise."

Dev cordially smiled his thanks to the appreciation of Shyam. After the dinner, Shyam requested Dev to accompany him to the Palace garden the next day.

"The King is interested to meet you, Dev," he said, "He wishes to listen to your flute in the royal garden."

Dev was silent for a moment. He looked troubled and uncertain. Shyam noticed his hesitation.

"Don't worry. You don't need to talk about your family, if you don't like it." He said again. "I have already told him about that. He is my friend, a man of understanding, and a lover of music. He is just interested in your music, you know."

As if a great burden was lifted from his heart. "That was so kind of you, Sir." Dev said with a sigh, "Life has spun a weird story around me, which was unfolded just a few days ago, you know. I need some time to adjust to it." He looked sad and lost as he stared far through the large windowpane.

Shyam patted him on his shoulder and said, "Though I don't know your predicament, I feel sorry for you. Sometimes we do need time to adjust to the veracities life presents us."

Dev looked at this kind friend with gratitude in his eyes. Shyam's understanding and affection reminded him of his father, he didn't know, why... He was deeply moved.

The next evening together they went to the Palace garden. Dev was surprised to learn that the garden adjacent to his room was indeed the royal garden. It was a vast stretch of land with mostly naturally grown trees and shrubs, decorated with fountains, statues, pebbled pathways and stone benches scattered around. The Palace guards saluted them as they entered the garden. The King was already waiting for them at the Marble Rock, they told.

Just adjacent to the Palace this place, known as the Marble Rock is the most beautiful spot in the garden. A naturally grown ridgeline of marble runs through the place, which was cut by the sculptors to design beautiful stone benches. An elevated platform was built beneath a shady banyan tree, which created a canopy of green overhead. There was a fountain formed within a huge marble lotus wonderfully sculptured in pink marble. Rocks of different shapes, sizes and colors were strewn around, enhancing the natural beauty of the place.

They found the King sitting beside the fountain on a couch covered with velvety red cushions. Dev bowed gracefully before the King. The King greeted them with a broad smile.

"So, you are Dev, the guest of my friend!" he said. "I'm glad to meet you." –

King Vikram was admiring the tall, beautiful physique and stately bearing of the handsome youth. He bade them to sit on the couches across the small tea table. After they became seated, an errand boy brought some refreshments of fruits, juices and sweets.

"Please help yourself." The King said with a warm smile. "You are the guest of my friend. You are my guest too."

"That's so kind of you, Your Majesty. Thank you." Dev said politely.

The cordial attitude of the King made Dev feel relaxed. He was admiring the beautiful sculptures around. The rays of the setting Sun created an unearthly splendor on the lotus made of veined pink marble. The fountain was beautiful with crystal clear water flowing around the lotus.

"I must say that I am impatient to listen to your flute, after we had had a glimpse of it yesterday." The King said after a while.

"I'm honored, Your Majesty." He said smiling. Taking out his flute, he lifted it to his lips and started to play. He was playing Raga Ahir-Bhairava. It was as delicate as the mist of the dawn on the Himalaya range. Starting on a low note, the music slowly gained its momentum. It expanded across the space like the gathering of clouds. The sound sometimes turned to be as poignant as a lover's longing and sometimes as somber and harmonious as the morning chants in the temple of Lord Shiva. The garden was enveloped in the enchanting sound of the music. The King and his friend, both were listening to it in deep admiration, with a sense of peace, joy and serenity flooding their hearts.

There was another one, who was listening to the music with rapt attention. It was the Princess. The sound of the music reached her in the Palace. Lila, feeling curious and drawn to it, came near the window of her room and found the musician sitting at a distance, on a couch in their Palace garden. In his fairly built form, absorbed in playing his flute, he looked like a god, like a sculpture in the temples. Listening to the sublime music her heart stopped. Who's this extraordinary musician? She was curious.

Even after Dev put the flute down, the music seemed to linger in the atmosphere. No one spoke for a long while.

"Wonderful!" said the King, breaking the silence, "I've never heard anyone play so well. I wish I could reward you for such a performance. But your music is truly priceless, young man."

"Thank you for your kind appreciation, Your Majesty." Dev said humbly.

"Will you please come to our garden and play for us every day, as long as you are staying here?"

"With pleasure, Your Majesty." Dev smilingly nodded his approval.

Shyam was very happy. Dev was his discovery. The music captivated him too, and he felt proud for him.

After Dev and Shyam left, Lila came to the garden and sat beside her father. "Lila Dear, today we had an exceptional musician here."

"I know; I too have heard him play the flute", Lila said calmly, hiding her excitement and admiration. "Who is he?" she pretended to ask casually, concealing her curiosity.

"I do not know much about him, Dear," said the King, "His name is Dev. He is from the village Mandira, presently staying with Shyam as his guest. Shyam speaks highly of the boy. He seems to be quite fond of the boy, you know."

Lila kept quiet.

"I have invited him to come to the royal garden to play his flute for us." The King said again. "Why don't you join us, Lila, tomorrow evening? You will enjoy the music, I am sure."

Lila was silent for a moment. She hesitated a little; she won't usually want to come out in public. But this flute player was really amazing.

She carefully restrained her excitement, though.

"Yes dad. That would be fine." She said.

On the way to their home, Dev inquired, whether Shyam had instructed his workmen to build the hut on the mountain near the cave of Sage Ramanam.

Shyam looked at Dev with embarrassment in his eyes. "I'm sorry, Dev. I forgot all about that", he said, "Tomorrow I'll order my people to go there and start building the hut."

"Please ask them not to delay", said Dev, "I just need a simple hut, with no extravaganza."

"I'll tell them about that", said Shyam, and they walked silently.

"You play your flute superbly, Dev," Shyam said after a while, "I've never listened to anybody playing such a sublime music, except Princess Lila."

Dev remembered that beautiful form and the sublime music he was fortunate to listen the first day he entered this city. However, he preferred to remain silent about that. He turned toward Shyam, curious to know more about her.

"She is our Princess, the only daughter of the King, you know," Shyam said, "She is an exceptionally gifted artist of Sitar, a natural born musician."

Dev was listening with quiet admiration. Shyam suddenly halted."Good God! I had forgotten... tomorrow afternoon I have an important meeting," he said. "Some royal dignitaries of the neighboring Kingdom are coming. If I am late, Dev, please go to the garden in time, in case His Majesty waits for you."

"Okay," Dev said hesitatingly, "but, will the Palace guards let me enter the garden?"

"Sure they will!" said Shyam, "They have seen me accompanying you."

Dev returned to his room. It was a moonlit night. He stood near the window. The royal garden was flooded with moonlight. The air was heavy with the delicate scent of some unknown night flower. Was it Champak or Kanchan? Why do they emit such fragrances in the night? He wondered. Do they worship their creator, unknowingly?

Many thoughts, many faces came crowding his mind. He remembered his village friends. He remembered Sania... Crazy girl! His heart became heavy at her memory. He was feeling grateful to that light-hearted village girl who made his gloomy days bright during his stay in the village. Dev didn't feel like sleeping. For a long time, he stood beside the window, motionless like a statue.

The Princess Promised

Shyam failed to turn up. He got caught up in the meeting as he apprehended. Evening was approaching. Dev was thinking if he should go to the royal garden. He must… in case the King was waiting there, like he did yesterday.

Dev took his flute and walked through the driveway toward the garden entrance. A Palace guard came running to him. "His Majesty is busy in a meeting," he said, making a respectful bow to Dev, "He bade you to wait for him at the Marble Rocks. Please come in."

The king was busy in the meeting. So, there was no hurry. Dev entered the Palace garden, and strolled around.

The moon was just coming out on the eastern horizon. It was a full moon night. The vast landscape was flooded with the mellow light of the moon. There were stone benches and fountains, decorated with lighted candles and colored glasses.

When Dev reached the Marble Rock, he was astonished to find a lady, probably a Palace maid, sitting there with her back facing him. It won't be polite to intrude on her privacy. He thought. He hesitated for a moment and decided to turn back.

Just at that moment, she turned around, and her gaze met his. He couldn't take his eyes away. Not only was she stunningly beautiful. A dignified elegance and poise wrapped her persona, making her look all the more gorgeous, like the snowy Himalayan summits look under the morning Sun. Dev felt a shiver run through his being. He had never felt like this before anybody else.

Innocence, wonder and command were mingled in her silent gaze. Could she be the Princess? Dev couldn't be sure, though he had probably seen her only a few days ago. The depth of her silent eyes and her charmingly poised persona seemed to cast a spell on him. He stood like a statue, unable to move, as if caught in a spell. He stared at her for several moments, almost falling into the depths of her charisma and then shook his head to recover.

"His Majesty bade me to wait here, Madam," He said finally regaining himself.

"Oh!" said the lady with a half smile, "You must be Dev."

Her voice was soft and melodious like the sound of a bell, but it was full of authority. Her heavenly beauty was radiating an aura of majesty.

"Your guess is right, Madam." Dev nodded, inwardly wondering how she came to know his name.

"I am Lila. Please be seated." said she.

"Good God, she is the Princess!" thought he. How come he couldn't recognize her, even after he saw her in the temple the other day? Dev rebuked himself. But the fault was not his. Today she appeared very different — much more beautiful and enchanting. That evening he saw her from a distance in the dim temple light, and today...

He couldn't think more. His heart was beating fast, he didn't know why. Dev presently joined her palms and bowed gracefully to her. She returned the bow gently folding her palms across her chest.

"I am glad to meet you, Your Highness." Dev said. The Princess smiled, gazing full on him.

Dev was looking for a bench to sit at a distance. The Princess showed him a bench nearby and bade him to sit there.

"Where did you learn playing your flute?" she said, reclining on her velvety couch. "I listened to it yesterday. It was wonderful."

"I learnt it from one of my friends at my teacher's house, Your Highness," Dev said briefly.

"Will you play your flute for me, till my dad and his friend come?" asked the Princess with command and request mingled in her clear voice.

"Sure!" Dev courteously smiled his consent. "I'll be honored to do the bidding of Your Highness". He said, taking the flute to his lips.

The music slowly soared high, as if, spreading its wings like a nightingale. After a while, it felt like floating above and below, enveloping the sky and valley in its silky, soothing embrace. Princess Lila was listening with rapt attention. She felt like the music carrying her over the hills and dales, above the mountain mists, above the rain clouds, high over the range of Himalaya to the abode of gods. She was overpowered by a feeling of unknown ecstasy. She was struggling inwardly to stay and look normal.

Dev was completely engrossed in his music. Everything disappeared for him — the Princess, the garden, the Palace, everything. After he stopped playing, he became conscious of the surrounding.

He found the Princess sitting motionless, gazing at a distance. Neither of them spoke a word for a while. Looking at her Dev couldn't quite guess if she liked his flute. Princess Lila appeared sober and reserved. Dev didn't dare to break her silence.

The Princess turned her gaze to him. "Superb!" She said in a measured tone, "I don't know how to reward you."

"Your appreciation is my reward, Your Highness. Thank you for your kind words." Dev said courteously, feeling very happy inside. – He could play his flute the whole night if she liked it, he thought secretly. — "It was my pleasure to play for you." He said again.

The Princess smiled. Her smile took him breathless.

"Your Royal Highness herself is an exceptional musician, I have heard." Dev said, gaining courage from her compliment. He didn't disclose that he listened to her in the temple.

"You must have learnt that from uncle Shyam," said the Princess. A small crease appeared on her smooth forehead. Dev wasn't sure if she liked this topic or not. But there was no going back. He quietly nodded, smiling.

She paused for a while and slightly bent her stately head, as if trying to decide whether to enter this discussion. A moment of uncomfortable silence passed.

"My music is nothing compared to yours." She said finally. "I play my sitar just because I love music, you know."

"I love music too, Your Highness; I just love to immerse myself in the melody of it." He said.

"Really! That makes you play it so well." She said smiling, presently putting aside her stately reserve.

"Doesn't everybody play music for the love of melody, Your Highness?"

"Yes, I think so," she said thoughtfully, "But I also play my sitar as an offering to God."

"Please forgive my ignorance, Your Highness," he said in innocent wonder, "Can it be satisfying to play music that way?"

The Princess looked amused. "Yes; melody is my vehicle to feel the presence of God."

"Really?" Dev was amazed. "Is it possible to feel the presence of God through music?" He wondered aloud, staring at her in admiration. In his wonder and amazement he forgot that gazing fully in the eyes of the Princess, and that too, a little known young lady, couldn't be considered very mannerly.

The Princess was amused at the simplicity and naiveté of this young man. "Yes... I can indeed feel the Presence, when I play my Sitar." She said.

Dev was captivated by the grace, dignity and the uncommon depth of the young Princess. The Vedas say, music is indeed the natural and most original expression of the Divine; but Dev, being an eminent scholar of the Vedas had never thought about this apart from mere academic interpretation. He was enamored by her wisdom. Dev desperately wished he could find a way to listen to her music again. "I wish, I could have the opportunity, Your Highness, to hear you play your Sitar", he said collecting much courage.

The Princess glanced at her hands, which were neatly folded on her lap. She was silent for a few moments. Dev kept quiet. May be he shouldn't have made such a request. After a while, she lifted her head and gazed at him.

"Okay…Your wish will be fulfilled," she said, with a half-smile playing on her lips. "Come here tomorrow afternoon." She paused for a moment, and added, "And don't forget to bring your flute."

This was beyond his dream. Dev could not conceal his excitement. A wide smile crossed his face. "Thank you," He said in delight, "I'll gratefully obey your will, Your Highness."

It had already been late in the evening. The King and his minister— none of them could make it here tonight. Dev took leave from the Princess and started to walk toward the house of the Prime Minister.

Shyam came back late in the night. He apologized for failing to turn up this evening. The King himself regretted, he said, for not being able to be present in the royal garden.

"It's alright." Dev said politely. They were dining together.

"You must have been tremendously bored, the whole evening sitting there all alone, waiting for us?" Shyam asked.

"Not at all," Dev said automatically. He was lost in his thoughts. He was thinking of the Princess, of her graceful manner, of her heavenly beauty and dignified bearing, and most of all, of the great depth of her personality. Suddenly he became conscious that Shyam was looking at him with surprise in his eyes.

Dev felt somewhat embarrassed and ashamed at his absent-mindedness.

"I was not alone, Sir." He said softly.

"You were not alone?" Shyam lifted his eyebrow.

"No, Sir. The Princess happened to be there, in the garden. She requested me to play the flute for her."

"Really! She is a great admirer of music, you know!" Shyam said, "In fact, yesterday I was thinking how happy she would be, if she listened to your music."

"Indeed she was!" Dev said, smiling. "Her Highness has invited me tomorrow afternoon, and she promised to play her Sitar too."

Shyam stopped eating and gazed fully at him. He was surprised beyond limit. This was very uncommon for the Princess. She always abhors playing before an audience. Dev was almost a stranger to her and a commoner. It is strange that the Princess would agree to play her Sitar before him. This boy seems to know magic; he thought, secretly smiling to himself.

"You are fortunate, Dev," he said openly, "because, the Princess never plays her music for anybody excepting the festive days in the temple."

Dev was silent. He was immersed in the memory of the evening, which appeared like a distant, sweet dream to him. Never in his whole life had he spent such an evening. Everything was so unusual, so wonderful. He was enthralled by the beauty, charisma, serenity and wisdom of the Princess.

"She is truly exceptional." Dev said unmindfully, as if thinking aloud. "My knowledge of the Vedas seems almost nothing to her natural wisdom."

Shyam kept staring at him, amazed. His guess was correct. The boy is erudite and talented. After the dinner was over, he took leave from Dev. "Tomorrow I, together with His Majesty, would surely like to join you, Young man". He said. Dev smilingly nodded.

In the Spell of Music

Sleep won't come to her tonight. The ethereal music of the flute, she heard in the evening, was still echoing in her ears. She was possessed by the music. Lila stayed awake in her room, quietly sitting beside the window. Looking outside, she saw the round moon suspending high above the sky.

Suddenly, she remembered his gaze. There was a tender kindness and pristine innocence in that gaze. Beauty, grace and nobility blended in his large deep eyes when he looked at her eyes. His high brow, broad and shining forehead, stately stature and polite demeanor spoke of his noble birth and education.

And what a dignified bearing! He should have been a Prince... But he could well be a recluse or a —a forest hermit as well. A gentle but awe-inspiring serenity surrounded him, as if nothing of this world matters to him. Silent admiration and subtle remoteness were mixed in his faraway gaze that told he does not belong to anything going on around him.

Suddenly Lila became alert that she had been thinking of the flute player. She was ashamed at the waywardness of her mind. But the man was really amazing; her mind said.

Lila had never met anyone like him. She had known men looking at her with awe, embarrassment and desire in their

eyes. No one had ever looked at her the way he did...
There was something wonderful in his charmed gaze. He
looked at her as though he was admiring the beauty of a
flower, or a mountain. –

His thought came to her over and over again. What is this?
She reproached herself. There is no reason that she should
keep thinking about a little known flute player.

Look, I'm certainly not thinking of a romantic
attachment— her mind reasoned with her— but I do think
that the man plays his flute exceptionally well. He is a
good flute player; that's all.

'Hmmm... but then, why can't you get him out of your
head?' A voice inside her asked. There was no answer.

When her reproach failed, she felt all the more
embarrassed. But she didn't give up. There is no point to
think about a man you know nothing about. 'Sure. The
man is a complete stranger.' The reasoning voice within
her said. 'I know nothing about him except his name.'

'So what?' A little voice within her head said, 'His
graceful attitude and stately demeanor speaks much about
him'.

Nothing seemed to work to silence her wayward mind.
'He is no ordinary flute player'; something kept
whispering within her. 'His music was superb, wonderful
and unparalleled. I wish I could hear him again and
again...'

The unruliness of her mind was beyond her control. This
was ever so unknown to her. Her thought went back in a

constant review of the evening. She had never met a man with so much charm and good looks. She couldn't help but think and ponder about this man, his wonderful voice, his dignified personality and artless simplicity.

The music won't leave her the whole of night and in the last half of the night she saw a strange dream. In her dream she saw the flute player playing his flute sitting on a boat. As she smiled, he smiled back, looking at her eyes. A shiver passed through her being. She was sitting on the bank of the river, listening to the music. Suddenly, she found the boat sailing away from her. The music faded away and his face became obscure. She woke up with an unknown pang in her heart.

She opened her eyes on her bed. Fresh morning air came to caress her face. The silk curtains of the windows were fluttering in the morning breeze. Birds were chirping in the garden and golden rays of the Sun came to her room heralding the beginning of a new day. Lila sat up over her bed. The ethereal music still lingered in her ears.

She walked up to the window and glanced out. Looking at the golden green leaves in the garden, she found a fine stream of happiness running through her being. Pushing the glass door open, she walked down the porch steps to have a stroll in the garden. Everything looked so perfect and beautiful. There was exhilaration in the air.

She was feeling very happy for no apparent reason. What's the matter? She covertly asked herself, inwardly reproaching her mind.

This is a beautiful day. See all the colors around you? —
Her mind said in defense. A small crease appeared on her
smooth forehead; she knew that there was more to it than
the simple happiness of walking in the garden on a sunlit
morning. To her embarrassment, she found herself waiting
for the Sun to go down.

##

Bella came late in the morning. She found the Princess lost
in her thoughts. They were sitting on the swing on the
porch. Lila was pretending to read the book in her hands in
an effort to hide her restlessness; but she couldn't
concentrate on it. She couldn't get the flute player out of
her mind.

"What happened to you, Lila?" Bella asked.

"Nothing," Lila snapped unmindfully, with a faraway gaze
in her eyes. She was afraid lest anybody knew what was
going on within her mind. Her abrupt reaction surprised
Bella. Lila felt a bit embarrassed too, sensing her surprise.
She took a deep breath and faced her friend. "I'm sorry,
Bella. I didn't mean to get short with you."

"I don't mind. But, won't you tell me what's it that's
troubling you?" Bella said. She was worried for her
beloved friend. She could see an unusual restlessness in
her that seemed to replace her usual calm.

"I myself don't know what it is." Lila said with a sigh. "I'll
tell you, Bella, when I understand it myself".

"You're trying to hide something from me, Lila. What makes you so restless today?"

"I really don't know, Bella…I—I mean I am not sure…"

Bella gazed at her friend with affection. She is very reserved about her feelings from her childhood; probably the sudden blow of losing her mother in an early age made her somewhat withdrawn and reserved about her feelings.

"Okay. Take your time and tell me, whenever you like. And let me know if I can be of any help."

Lila glanced gracefully at her friend. She mildly caressed her hand. "Thank you, Bella, for being patient with me," she said. "Let's go to the garden." She stood up and walked down the porch steps. Her friend joined her and they strolled down the sidewalk in the Palace garden.

"You see, Bella, I'm not hiding anything." Lila said again, in her defense. "I am just a bit confused and perplexed myself…"

Bella kept quiet. She could understand that something was troubling her friend, which she was denying even to herself. She was sorry to see her struggling within herself.

The Horse Found Its Owner

Late in the morning Dev was returning from the river after his daily meditation. Coming near the Palace gate he found men, women and children running. What's the matter? A crease appeared on his forehead. Within a short while he knew what it was.

A stallion, fierce-eyed, nostrils wide, foams falling from its mouth was running wildly hither and thither, scaring people on the way. It was dark black in color; its long tail and thick mane were tossing around its unruly head. The horse must have broken loose from the royal stable.

There were a few carriages that stopped at a distance sensing danger. Quickly Dev decided what he had to do. He took the fine cotton cloth covering the upper part of his body, tightly tied it around his slender waist and waited for the horse to come near him.

Just as the horse came near him, he stood aside swiftly, got hold of its rein and jumped on its back. The graceful movement of the action startled everybody standing nearby. The stallion got aggressive and furiously stood on its hind legs trying to fling him off its back. Dev held the lasso forcefully with the grasp of his master hand, bent his supple body on its back and put his legs tightly around its waist. In storms of wrath, rage and fear, the savage stallion furiously circled the place and reared again, trying to shake him off. Becoming unsuccessful in its attempt the hot steed galloped away with Dev on its back.

This incident created quite a stir among the people. It was also witnessed by some courtiers coming to the Palace in their carriages. Their breaths stopped as the daring youth jumped on the back of the maddened beast, putting his life in danger.

They were anxiously discussing it among them, when King Vikram and his Prime Minister arrived at the court. The King ordered his horse-riding soldiers to go in the direction the horse took the stranger away.

There was furrow on Prime Minister Shyam's forehead. He didn't see Dev in the morning. Could it be he? He dismissed the thought in a trice. That was not possible. Dev is a scholarly person, perhaps from a noble Brahmin family. It is very unlikely for him to do that.

Everyone in the court was waiting in suspense. A foreign merchant sold this horse only a month before. It is a stallion of Arabian breed, deep black in color with silky shine on its skin; with its delicate head, strong neck and expressive wide-set eyes, it made a good impression on all. Its owner spoke highly about its stamina and agility. The King admired the horse and bought it for five hundred gold coins. They named it Rupak.

However, the horse turned to be absolutely unruly. It has already shaken off its back two eminent Generals of the army, both men of prowess. They have survived with minor injuries. Nobody dared to ride on its back, since then.

This morning the horse accidentally broke loose from the royal stable. In the court everybody waited in suspense, anxious about the fate of the stranger.

##

The horse was galloping away on the wide pastures, with Dev firmly seated on its back, holding its rein in his tight fists. He was feeling relieved at the thought of averting the imminent danger. The road in the morning was busy and filled with carriages and pedestrians— men, women and children, going about their work. If the horse was not driven away, anything could happen.

He didn't worry about himself. He was a master in handling horses. He knew much about these stallions of Arab breed. They not only possess beauty and nobility, but also a rare combination of strength and intelligence. Respect, once earned by the handler, would always be with these stallions. Once they accepted someone as their master, they would remain fiercely loyal, obedient and reliable even in the most demanding circumstances.

On the wide pastures, the stallion broke in to a powerful trot, exhibiting strength and aggression. Dev was just waiting for the horse to get tired. After a long while the stallion slowly turned to a rhythmic, floating trot. Dev knew that this was the opportune moment. He tightly held the rein in his one hand and with his other hand he patted on its neck, calming it with words of assurance in a soothing voice.

Dev had known from his experience that horses have a keen instinct to sense the intention of its handler and they usually respond to good intention and affection. He knew that he needed to treat it respectfully to make it feel at home. He laid his palm softly across its eyes and drew it gently down its neck and panting flanks. He softly spoke to it, assuring that it need not fear.

The stallion seemed to respond to his words of affection. It further slowed its pace and began to respond to the slightest pull of the rein. Dev breathed a sigh of relief. Now it was a joy to ride on its soft broad back with its lively gait. He was ready to take it back to the Palace. Just at that moment, he saw two soldiers coming his way on their horses. They came near him and stopped. Dev stopped the stallion with slightest pull of the rein. They looked at the stallion and then they looked at him with wide-eyed awe and wonder.

"Sir, His Majesty is anxiously waiting for you in the court. He bade us to take you there." This was all they could say.

Approaching the Palace Dev found the Palace guards and attendants staring at him with awed admiration; the stallion carrying him was looking tame and docile like a trained pony. The royal guards recognized him at once and news reached the court that the stranger was none other than the guest of the Prime Minister. They said he was back hale and hearty, riding the wild horse, now tamed by him.

King Vikram was surprised. Prime Minister Shyam was astonished too. A mixed feeling of wonder, admiration and affection flooded their hearts.

In front of the royal court, Dev jumped down from the horseback. The royal horse-trainer came running to him. The horse was standing subdued and meek, sinking its proud crest low. Dev patted the horse on its neck and softly spoke to its ears. He gave the rein to the royal trainer and said, "Treat him with love and respect; he will obey."

A royal attendant led him to the court hall. All the eyes were upon him. Beauty, nobility and intelligence were shining on his stately appearance. His unkempt hair, broad forehead, calm countenance, wide chest, and confident stride radiated a rare combination of courage, strength and poise.

Shyam rose from his seat and greeted him. "Bravo, my young friend! You have saved our people from danger," he said, "I feel proud of you."

"I consider myself fortunate to be able to be at your service, honorable Sir!" Dev said humbly. He smiled his thanks to the Prime Minister and then he turned to greet the King and the court with a gracious bow.

King Vikram was visibly moved in admiration for this noble youth. "I never knew, young man, that a Vedic scholar and talented flute player could also be an expert in taming the wild horses!" He said, with a smile of appreciation."Will you mind disclosing your secret of taming the fierce horse?"

Dev smiled humbly. "Courage, patience, love, and will are my secrets, Your Majesty," he said respectfully.

"No praise and no tribute is enough to reward your strength, valor and noble spirit, young man," said the King to the joy and applaud of all, "I wish to gift Rupak, the stallion to you as a sign of my gratitude for saving my subjects from the danger."

Dev was feeling embarrassed for such words of praise and more so for the reward. He had done what anybody at his place would do to avert the danger.

"I'm grateful for your kindness and generosity, Your Majesty; but, I've merely done what I felt was my duty," he respectfully said to the King, "I earnestly entreat you not to give me the horse, or any gift, for that matter. Your Majesty knows I am staying as a guest of the honorable Prime Minister, and my kind friend provides everything I need."

Dev paused with a grin of gratitude at Shyam, to which he responded with a smile of affection. The King and his court were further impressed at the dignity and graciousness of the young man.

"Okay. Then, I will send the horse to Shyam." The King said, and before Dev could say anything, he said again, "Today the horse has found its master in you, Dev. It will be happy to have you ride on it. Please don't deny." The courtiers joined their hands in applause. Dev became instantly popular among them. He accepted the gift with a gracious bow.

The news of this uncommon event reached the inner chambers of the Palace too, and created a silent stir among the Palace maids and attendants.

##

Bella was watching her friend with concern. They were sitting together, but Lila was not her usual self. Now she looked restless, and a moment later she was still, lost in her thoughts and disinterested in whatever was happening around her. Bella could not make out what happened to her.

A while ago, when Dev alighted from the stallion, Lila saw him from a Palace window. She was sitting near the window. When she saw a young man on a steed coming down the road toward the Palace, she thought he looked like Dev, simply because he'd been on her mind a lot. Then, as he got closer, she realized that it was indeed him. At the first instant Lila couldn't believe her eyes. When and where did he possibly learn to ride a steed? And what on earth was he doing there, with the King and the ministers in the court?

She was further surprised to see his appearance. He looked regal and graceful on the horseback. His sweated forehead was half covered with unruly hairs; his shapely form was visible, with his bare chest wide open and the upper garment tightly tied around his waist. He looked like a Greek god coming alive from the pages of a mythological story.

Her heart was beating fast at the sight of him. Lila was feeling really confused and tired, unable to reason with herself why the mere sight of this man should cause such a stir of emotion within her. She went on the terrace adjacent to the garden, feeling somewhat restless. Bella came and sat beside her after a while.

Bella was trying hard to make her speak out. Lila was sitting very still, listlessly staring at the Palace garden. She looked thoughtful.

Mitra, the Palace maid came running with amazement, awe and excitement written on her face.

"What happened, Mitra?" asked Bella.

"....I'd been there at the Palace kitchen...... and Jaya came there with the news.....I heard....we all heard....this was incredible....." She faltered.

"What's it?" Bella was curious.

"He seems to know spell." She gulped, "or, maybe, he has the powers of the gods."

"Who is it? Don't make a riddle, Mitra." Bella said impatiently in a reproaching tone.

"The young gentleman, I don't remember his name, the guest of our Prime Minister..." Mitra said breathlessly. She seemed to lose her words in excitement.

Suddenly the Princess became alert, eager and attentive.

"What happened to him?" she asked casually, trying to conceal her eagerness and curiosity.

"Our Rupak, the wild stallion broke loose from the royal stable, Your Highness. It was running helter-skelter on the street, threatening the life of people." Mitra said. "This stranger appeared on the spot, God knows from where, held it on its rein, hopped on its back and disappeared." She paused to catch her breath.

"Then what happened?" Lila said anxiously. Bella was staring at her, surprised to note her friend's interest in such a trivial incident.

Lila ignored the surprised glance of her friend. "Tell us whatever you know about this." she said again, turning to the maid.

Mitra described in details how the stranger put his life to risk to ride the fierce beast; she told them about the worry of the King and the ministers about his safety. And she narrated with obvious delight how the man came back victorious riding the fierce horse looking docile as a deer with him on its back. She told them about the King's praise, his generous gift, and of the man's humble decline to accept the King's offer. Mitra was enthused to recount the story. Both the friends were listening, holding their breath.

"Is he safe?" Lila interrupted Mitra.

"Yes my Princess, he is without a trace of injury, I can swear; he is very brave and strong, and he's got extraordinary power, Your Highness." Mitra paused to catch her breath. "But His Royal Majesty made him accept the gift finally. 'The horse has found his master,' our King said." The maid concluded, by picking up the thread of the story from where she had been distracted.

Lila took the gold necklace off her neck and presented it to the maid, who was pleasantly surprised and obliged to have the unexpected gift from the Princess .   She bowed to them and left.

"What is it, Lila? Why did you give your necklace to her?" asked Bella with a grin. She was surprised beyond limit.

"I gave it to her because she told me a story that gladdened my heart." Lila said with a mysterious smile playing on her lips.

Bella frowned at this. She could not make out why her friend was so much interested to learn the story of a stranger. Granted, the story was interesting, and such a thing does not happen every day. But that did not explain why her dear friend would be so concerned over the safety of a stranger.

The Flower Blossomed

It was a long day. Lila was impatient. When will the evening come? She could not concentrate in anything she was doing. She grew more restless with the approach of the afternoon. Now she picked up a book and turned her attention to the words on the page in front of her in an effort to drive him off her mind. She read the first sentence three times before she realized that, though she was reading it, she really didn't know what it said. Oh God…What was wrong with her? This was ridiculous.

For the tenth time she went to her window to glance down to the garden. This was ridiculous too. She smiled at herself. God…! Where did her sober sense go? What the Palace attendants are there for? Won't they inform her if he came?

Walking up to her dressing mirror unmindfully she ran the brush through her curly hair. A crease appeared on her smooth forehead again. Why did she even care about how she appeared? This was a stranger, a musician who was coming at her bidding to play his music for her, the Princess of the land.

'Not exactly. He is coming to listen to my Sitar...' A part of her mind mused.—

'Well, agreed. But why on earth should that excite me?' Lila frowned again. Admiration and praise for her music wasn't new to her... She kept the brush back in the drawer.

Lila looked at the clock. Soon he was going to come. Unable to reason with herself, she gave up at last, and asked a maid to take her Sitar to the garden. She smiled to herself. She doesn't even know the man; yet her pull to him was so strong. This was something unknown to her so far.

He found her sitting on the stone platform beneath a shady tree with her eyes closed and her stately neck slightly bent, immersed in playing her sitar. Dev took a deep breath cautiously, lest he disturbed her.

But he could not resist his eyes stealing through the beauty of her enthralling presence. An ivory white silk gracefully clad her person. Curly hairs surrounding that beautiful face covered part of her pearly white forehead, like the black clouds cover the snowy Himalayan summits in the monsoon. They went down long past her shoulders. Her long and shapely fingers were gracefully moving on her Sitar.

She wasn't wearing any special jewelry today; only a single strand of pearl bracelet was visible around her flawless wrist. Dev couldn't believe how naturally pretty she was. She looked like a goddess immersed in her worship. The rich and sweet tone of her Sitar was filling the air.

His heart seemed to stop. Dev held his breath in deep admiration of the heavenly beauty of the Princess. He sensed a faint fragrance of Jasmine in the air.

Looking around, he spotted a marble bench at a distance from the Princess. He walked over to it to take his seat and tried to concentrate on the music.

Taking a slow deep breath, Dev closed his eyes and started listening to the music. She was playing an enchanting tune.

What raga was she playing? He tried to focus his mind. Slowly he was caught in its tempo. The pure melody of her sitar was flowing like a great river rushing through the hills and the valley, gathering momentum as it progressed, sweeping everything on its way.

It covered the whole valley, the earth and the heaven. Whatever it touched seemed to glow with radiant bliss. The music touched his heart too, as if waking it up from its slumber of sadness. He sat enchanted, with a feeling of deep peace and joy enveloping his being— a feeling that disappeared from his life from the fateful day his father disclosed the queer story of his life.

After she stopped playing her Sitar, the Princess opened her eyes and softly gazed at the forest of Pines and Deodars on the horizon. Dev was feeling a thrill enveloping his being; the music still seemed resonating in the air. He did not feel like breaking the silence, which seemed almost sacred.

"Your music was truly divine, Your Highness." He tenderly said after a while. "I consider myself privileged, you know, to be present here today to listen to this."

The Princess turned toward him and smiled gracefully without saying anything. For a moment his heart felt as if it stopped beating.

"I've kept my promise. Now play your flute for me." She said.

Dev took his gaze away from her and glanced down for a moment. "I feel at a loss, Your Highness, about what tune to play after this." He said benignly, looking up to the Princess. "Your music was truly humbling."

"Play what you like; I'd love to listen to it." She insisted.

Dev took his flute to his lips. After listening to the sublime music of the Princess, he was feeling very peaceful and relaxed. He poured his heart in his flute.

The melodious music of his flute floated in the air. It started to flower like a lotus in the bloom; it was so delicate, so soft and enchanting. The music stirred something deep within her. Lila could almost see a flower of thousand petals blossoming; the petals were opening, one after another, to ultimately reveal its soft silky bosom. The flower enveloped the valley with its unearthly radiance. It unfolded its wondrous petals in her heart too, to take her completely within its blissful corona. She was struggling to hide her ecstasy and look normal.

Time stopped on the valley. She sensed a subtle bliss surging up, dissolving her from within. A deep and rich silence came over the garden, when the music came to halt. The atmosphere was almost electrifying. Occasionally, the hush of the breeze blowing through the trees and shrubs was breaking the somber silence of the night. The moon shone bright in the spotless autumn sky.

"Your music is magical. It's something I can bet my life for…" She said; her voice deep and mellow.

Dev felt a shiver mixed with wonder, awe and ecstasy passing through him. He hoped she won't notice it.

"Thank you, Your Highness; I'm glad that you liked it." He said, hiding his excitement.

The Princess didn't seem to notice what he said.

"I won't hesitate to give you away whatever you want for playing it to me every day of my life." She said again, taking a deep breath.

Dev was startled again.

"The music is yours to call upon, Your Highness, whenever you wish," he said courteously.

She bit the inside of her lip. "And what about the musician?" she asked, pretending innocence.

"I— I beg your pardon?"

"What if I want to own the musician too?" She asked again in a cajoling voice.

Stunned, Dev looked at her. Did she mean to say that she was interested in him? Nah, it's impossible. She must be joking.

"Your Royal Highness is joking, I suppose." Dev leaned back in his seat, smiling.

"No," she nodded in disapproval. "I'm not joking. I'm serious. What if I want to own the musician too along with his music?" She said again, her voice unwavering.

'The musician is yours forever.' Dev wished to say. However, presently he decided to pretend naïve again. She was the Princess of the land, and him, an unknown youth…just a commoner. How can he dare to think that she might be interested in him? He desperately strove to keep himself away from the radiant flower of passion that started blossoming in his heart.

"Thank you, Your Highness, if you've kindly offered me the job of royal musician." He said openly, gazing up to her. "But, I came to the city with a different purpose, you know."

The Princess shook her head causing her hair to catch the moonlight. She was looking majestic, fascinating and breathtakingly beautiful. Dev sensed his heart stop beating.

"No, no, no; I am not offering you the position of the royal musician either." She said in desperation, all the while placing her gaze on him.

"But I—I don't understand, Your Highness," he faltered.

"I said… I want to own the musician, who also happens to be an expert in taming fierce and wild horses…" She said again taking her gaze away and glancing down. She fiddled with a golden thread in her cloth for a while.

Dev was completely clueless and at a loss about what to say. Was he dreaming? Is she real or a dream vision? He was staring helplessly at her.

The Princess covertly smiled at his helpless look. "...Hope I've made it clear enough..." She lowered her voice glancing down and bit her lip. "I want to have exclusive possession of the musician... forever..." She whispered again in a soft tone. Now she was gazing fully at him.

A shiver passed through his being. She did make it clear as crystal. He sensed a strange rapture in his heart, as he was gazing in to those beautiful eyes. But this was beyond his wildest dream. He'd been caught by her grace and enchanting persona; but a shadow of doubt hovered in his mind. –Does she really know what her words mean? Or, was she just playing with her words? Or worse, could it be just a whim, as Princesses are often known to have?

No, No; that is absolutely not possible. — Dev reproached himself inwardly for thinking this. She can't be telling this frivolously. Such a music as hers can't emerge of a frivolous heart and unthinking mind. May be she is really meaning what she is saying?

Dev felt confounded about how to respond back. Sure... This was walking on the razor's edge. A faintest error of judgment can prove fatal. He made up his mind. He won't yield to her unless he was sure that she meant what she said. —

She was staring at him for his reply. Dev took his eyes away from her.

"Perhaps you don't know what you say, Your Highness..." He said reticently.

"I know;" interrupted she; she did not take her gaze off his countenance all the while. "I know what I said and I mean it." She said again and paused for a moment, taking her gaze down.

Dev was silent. A sea of wild emotions was surging in his heart. He wished to say how deeply he loved and adored her, but could not say anything. He kept quiet. Part of him could not believe what was happening.

A few moments of electrifying silence passed. The Princess let her fingers play a little with the strings of her Sitar. Then she lifted her head, gazing full at his eyes.

"Your music stirred my soul like no one and nothing did. I tried hard to conceal that from everyone, you know, even from me; but I failed." She smiled. The immaculate splendor of that smile enthralled his mind. He stared at her as if spellbound.

The Princess took her soft gaze away from him to look at a distance for a moment and then glanced at him again.

"I struggled much against myself, you know; but my mind won't cooperate;" she said with a piteous smile, "and now, I'm here at the mercy of a stranger, who took my heart completely in his captivity." She paused and rested her eyes silently upon him waiting for his reply.

In the moonlight her ivory-white dress, captivating smile and ethereal beauty dazzled his eyes and enchanted his mind. She looked like an angel coming up from the pages of a fairytale. It was impossible to resist her. Dev felt waves after waves of love surging within his heart which, if he let loose, would be beyond his control.

But there was another turmoil going on deeper within his mind. The thought of his unknown ancestry was haunting him, driving him crazy. 'You can never expect to be loved, so long you carry this deep wound within your heart;' a little voice within his head said. 'How can you hope to be accepted and respected when you yourself have little self-esteem left within?'

She was quietly waiting for his reply. Dev was feeling helpless and restless, not knowing how to thwart the surge of deep love welling up within his heart. But what will she think when she comes to know more about him?

However, his heart had already surrendered to her, failing all the resistance his mind posed. Softly he gazed at her eyes. "This stranger too reciprocates your feelings, my dear Princess, and feels immensely happy and grateful to surrender in your captivity." He said.

Her radiant face beamed with a beautiful smile and she appeared much relieved. Dev paused for a moment to admire her face, now glowing with gentle love.

"I don't understand how you could want me, but the fact that you do makes me feel blessed. I've come to adore you from the moment I've seen you in the temple, you know," he said again, smiling diffidently. "I've never told you that…"

"You cheat!" Lila smiled too and frowned, pretending anger. "I thought you've never listened to my music."

"I've never said that." Dev said in his defense, smiling again. "I just said I wished to listen to it, and I meant I wished to listen to it again, and again and again!"

"Really! I never knew then in the temple that someone was waiting there to steal my heart away!" She said smiling shyly.

"True; but today your music has completely swept me away, my sweet Princess. My heart has been yours forever…" He said sweetly.

A stream of subtle happiness was running through him. But his mind won't let him bask in that joyful feeling. 'You must tell her everything about yourself, even at the risk of losing her love;' it kept haunting him.

Sure, — he thought— I must be true to her. I must tell her everything about myself.

The Princess was staring at him with her soft expectant gaze and gentle smile. Dev smiled faintly, gazing at her.

"But you practically know nothing about me." Dev said again, crossing his arms across his chest. "How could you love me without ever knowing anything about me? You don't know who I am; you don't know which family I belong to…"

"I don't care to know," she interrupted. She came down from her platform to sit on the bench close to him. "Your heavenly music, your graceful demeanor, your courage, skill and noble spirit speak enough about you." She said smiling. "I love you and not your lineage, you know."

Dev shook his head in desperation.

"But I can't rest until I tell you everything, Dear Princess. Destiny has weaved a strange story around me..." He said.

She seemed to take little notice of what he said. "Lila." she said, smiling; "My name is Lila; call me by that."

Dev glanced at her, his gaze full of affection and admiration. She is stunningly beautiful, fascinating and— he thought with a secret smile of fondness— and... a little crazy. She was staring at him, waiting for his response.

Dev hesitated for a moment and then relented to her wish. "Okay; Lila." He said smiling. In the moonlight their laughter mingled to form a glad symphony.

"Now tell me your story," she said in an intimate voice, "but, not as an excuse to escape from my captivity; I'd love to share your hopes, your dreams your life and your aspirations."

They were gazing at each other's eyes. The evening moon was gently smiling on them. "I love you, my sweet Princess," Dev whispered. Lila smiled, but couldn't say anything. She was on the top of her world feeling so light and relieved, being in such nearness to the man she came to love so deeply.

The stress of the past few days, of fighting with her own mind had wearied her down. The stress of this evening, of expressing her mind to him was not any less either. And now that she knew for certain that she won his heart, all her stress flew away. She was feeling utterly relaxed. She was floating on the silent bliss welling up in her heart.

He kept gazing at her eyes for a few moments, admiring her breathtaking beauty and her pristine innocence. Only if he could make this moment last forever; he sighed. But the bizarre story of his life must be told. He cleared his throat and sighed again.

He told her about his Brahmin father, pious mother, of his pride of his clan and his small village Mandira.

"Have you ever been to the countryside?" He asked her.

She shook her head. "I've only lived in this capital city all my life, but I've heard it is really pretty."

Dev nodded in agreement. "It is, just like you." He said earnestly, and smiled at her scarlet blush.

Princess Lila was thoroughly enjoying his story. Reliving the bygone days in his memory now his eyes lit up with a strange light and the next moment his countenance was pale with a sad smile.

Gazing deeply in to her beautiful eyes, Dev found nothing but care and compassion. He made up his mind. He would withhold nothing from her. He would let her share every bit of his life— all his joys and all his pain. He won't hide anything from her.

Dev told her about his unknown lineage and parentage. He ran his hand through his hair in deep anguish and frustration and kept silent for a moment. Lila was silent too, her gaze blended with gentle love.

"That uncanny evening, took everything away from me, Lila — everything— my life, my self-esteem and my pride as an erudite Brahmin scholar." He said, a sigh of deep anguish storming his heart. "Just a few days ago life was full of certainties for me, you know. I believed in myself and I believed in whatever I studied in the Vedas." He muttered, reminiscing his happy days in his village. "I was held in respectful adoration by my mates and students alike, and was about to start my own school. That cursed evening destroyed everything. It shattered all my beliefs and all my dreams. It robbed me off my identity, pride and dignity, you know." A deep sigh came out of him.

Lila came closer to him, reached for his arm and patted him with deep affection.

"Your story is truly stirring, my love," She said softly, "But, I don't see anything in it that could bother you so much."

"Really?" He stared at her uncertainly for a few moments. Then he lowered his head, as if to hide the deep agony that tormented his soul.

"Nobody in the world knew my story, except my foster parents." He said again as he sighed and rubbed his temples. "But I had to be true to myself, you know. I could not pretend to be a Brahmin scholar and live with ease in a society that highly upholds the caste system and hold the Brahmins in the highest honor. Nor could I degrade myself in the eyes of people by disclosing my unknown parentage. The only choice I was left with was to abandon my home and village…"

Lila was feeling deep admiration for this man. What an exceptional integrity and strength of character he possesses! Her heart was glad that she loved this man.

"We can do nothing, Dev, about where we are born, you know." She said.

He sighed again gazing at her eyes. The subtle tenderness and compassion in her gaze melted his heart.

"So you say Lila, my dearest," he said, "but our village society won't appreciate that. Nor would my mind listen to me. Was I a stray child born of the entertainment of a man and a woman? Even today this thought drives me almost crazy, you know." Dev fought back his tears. He was scared lest they come out in full force to make him more vulnerable. His eyes were burning.

He looked up feeling a gentle touch on his arm, and smiled softly at her. "Don't say that, Dear." She whispered as she reached up and straightened out the sleeves of his shirt. "You are surely born of a noble family. I've no doubt about that. Your integrity, courage and strength of character tell that."

"I'm ever grateful to you, my love, for your understanding..." he said, as he brushed a few stray curls out of her face. "But, you know, I feel restless to find out if there really was a respectable hereditary lineage that I could boast about, but I'm clueless about how to do that."

"Your foster parents have taken care of you since when you can remember. They are your parents in their own right, dear."

Dev shook his head. "That's not my point, Lila. I feel
deeply indebted to them, probably more so than when I
believed they were my real parents."

"Then where's the problem, dear?"

"That weird story destroyed all my pride and self-worth,
you know. It has made me a subject of self-pity." He said
with a sigh.

She was anxious to see his sadness. "Sometimes things
keep happening to us on which we have no control, Dev."

He did not seem to listen to her. "But I really don't possess
an identity, you see." He said in anguish. "Neither can I
remain true as the Brahmin son of a Brahmin father; nor
do I know whether I really belong to the warrior caste,
which my foster father guesses."

"I don't care." She frowned and smiled. "I don't care
about your family or your past; you are enough as you are.
I feel blessed to have you in my life."

"But, I care, Lila! How can I rest in peace when I don't
have an identity? I want to find my identity in this
universe." He said in despair.

Her soft, expectant gaze fell upon his. There was nothing
but love and admiration in her silent admiring gaze,
though. His light brown wavy hair, handsome features and
stately stature attracted her from the moment she saw him.
He is refined, dignified and graceful. Much more so than
anybody else she ever met. The admiring gaze of his large
dark eyes and deep, sonorous voice stirs something deep
within her. And just now she came to know about the

amazing integrity of his character. This was the man she waited all her life for.

"You are the greatest blessings that life has ever brought to me, dear." She whispered after a while. "In fact unless things had been like they are, I could have never found you." She said again.

Dev took a deep breath. Her loving words and presence were removing the gloom from his heart.

"I feel blessed too, you know, to have you in my life..." He said tenderly, taking her hands in his. "Your love has tremendously enriched my life... But when a man loses his self-worth, he loses everything, you know...." He paused with a sigh.

"Why are you worried about something that is beyond your control?" Lila sounded impatient. "Can't you move past those memories?"

Dev shook his head in desperation.

"Can't my love fill up the void in your life, Dev?" Lila came closer to him. Dev could almost feel her breath.

"It surely can, sweetheart; I can't deny. That's the most amazing thing that ever happened to me...That's the only silver lining in my gloom." He said gazing fully in her eyes. "But that doesn't erase the wacky feeling of worthlessness..." He sighed.

Lila kept quiet. An unknown pang was making her feel restless.

"I love you too with all my heart." He said again. "But I don't know how to silence those weird thoughts that cripple my mind. It seems I can't find rest till I find who I am."

"What do you want to do?"

He looked above to the shining moon. "Oh God!" He mumbled, as if to himself. "Only if I knew a way out of this strange predicament..." He sighed and turned to the Princess. "I know I may need to tear my heart away and leave it to you, if I want to pursue my search." He whispered.

Lila was stunned. "Pursue your search...???" She repeated. "Do you plan to go away from me? Will you leave us, Dev?" Her voice trembled and her soft lips quivered as she grabbed his arm.

Dev felt the powerful stream of love surfacing up and overpowering him with its mighty flow.

"I won't, dear, if you don't permit," he said in a voice of surrender. "I'll do whatever you want." He promised.

She said nothing. Her eyes were full of tears.

"But this damned feeling of rootlessness is eating me up..." He muttered again, as if to himself.

"Who says you are rootless?" Lila said in an assuring tone. "You do have a good family, a noble upbringing and a wonderful educational background, Dev."

Dev took his head within his hands and lowered it in desperation. "So you say, dear, because you love me." He said lifting his head and smiled piteously looking at her. "I love you too, and I'll continue to love you till I die. Your

love's the most wonderful and precious thing that destiny
has brought to this hapless man…"

Lila felt sorry at his self-pity. But there was nothing she
could do to remove it. Both remained silent for a moment.
Only the rustling sound of leaves in the breeze was
breaking the somber silence of the night.

"I'm like a lost ship, you know, in this vast ocean of life."
He whispered dejectedly as if to himself, gazing at the
star-studded sky. "Why, whatever I've done in my life so
far seems like a big zero."

Lila said nothing. She became very still and quiet. A surge
of tears welled up in her heart and numbed her limbs. But
she could see the tremendous unrest within him; an unrest
that would never allow him to be his usual self...

"True love demands merging of selves, Lila," he
whispered again, breaking the silence; "but, which self do
I bring to you, dear? My old self, the scholar and erudite
Brahmin Dev died long ago, the day my father told me my
bizarre story. And the Dev you see in front of you is like a
tree without any root, like a shadow without any
substance. I have no identity, no self that I can hold on to.
Can you see my hopelessness?" He paused and rubbed his
temples. A deep sigh came from his heart.

"I can feel your pain, dear. But don't be so upset." Lila
said softly. Her tearful eyes were filled with a soothing
light of compassion. "I love you as you are now; I'm not at
all concerned with your past."

His heart melted. "Dev is eternally grateful to you." He
whispered and shook his head in frustration. "But I can

hardly explain what is going on within me, sweetheart. My education and my pride in my heritage seems to mock me. The blood running in my vein feels like poison… Your love irresistibly attracts me toward you and my low self-worth repels me from myself. I'm being torn inside." He sounded inconsolable.

"Strange are the ways of the destiny, you know. Don't regret because you lost your old identity. Perhaps future holds a grander promise for you, dear."

"Perhaps;" Said Dev. "But I need to find my self-worth, dear, before I find any rest in my heart."

"A man is much better defined by his deeds rather than his birth; I think." Lila said, mildly pressing his hands.

"It isn't as simple as you say, dear. A man's identity is a much more complex thing." Dev said standing up and stretching his hands upwards toward the heaven. "I want to know… Does the name and lineage of a family make up all there is to it to speak of a man? Or, is there anything else that defines our existence on earth more perfectly, more conclusively, more coherently? I want to know if there is truly any such place where man eternally belongs." He said with a faraway gaze in his eyes, as if speaking to himself.

His restlessness was evident as he paced to and fro in front of her, with his hands crossed on his chest.

Lila knew he was searching for the answers to the questions regarding his unknown birth — the questions that tormented his soul.

"Do you believe in the immortality of the self?" He suddenly asked her.

"All selves are mortal, Dev;" She said calmly. "Only Love is immortal. It is the place in our heart where we truly belong."

"If Love is immortal, how can we mortals relate to it? Does it create our destiny? Then why do humans suffer? Then what defines such torments as I'm going through in this life?"

"I don't know all the answers to your questions, Dev; but this much I know: 'Love' is all in all and it can erase all our karma, when one truly surrenders to it. I'm referring to the word in a much grander sense, of course." She said.

Dev stared at her with an admiring gaze. "You are much wiser than I am," He said.

"Really? You really think I am?" She said with a light voice, wishing to lighten the atmosphere.

"Yes, you are." He said smiling, coming over to her.

"Then give me my reward!" She whispered.

He held her face in his hands and stared at her for a while. She shivered at his touch. He sensed her shiver and his blood ran fast in his heart. He wished to hold her in close embrace, but finally he decided to let go of her.

She looked down disappointed, and her lower lip trembled, making Dev feel bad. "Truly I don't deserve you," he said in deep anguish as he tried to pull apart. "My mind is scattered and fragmented. Do you think I can fulfill you, my love? I doubt…"

He felt the pull of her hands, tightly clinging to his shirt. He couldn't help smiling. Clinging to him with both her hands she looked like a baby— pure, guileless and innocent. He grabbed her and wrapped her in a hug. "I love you... I helplessly love you." He whispered in her ear.

She gave him a tearful smile. "I love you too."

"I don't know what I've done to gain such precious love..." he said gazing at her eyes in deep gratitude. "I'm really hopeless to ever contemplate of leaving you for my search."

"Isn't it possible to stay back and continue your search?" She asked in innocence.

"I think there's nobody except the sage who can pull me out of my restlessness, dear..." He said. "Because I want to find the answers to my questions not from the pages of scriptures— I had studied enough of them. Nor do I want to learn it from the vain utterances of the pundits and scholars— I had been one of them. I want to find it from my own experiential understanding. If I don't find a satisfactory answer to my questions, my present existence will continue to haunt me as a meaningless nonsense that can come to no use to anybody on earth." He sighed.

Lila kept quiet. Silent tears were filling her oceanic eyes. Her heart shrank in trepidation. Her shoulders slumped. Dev was watching her.

He felt an urge to hold her face in his hands again to wipe her tears, but he resisted himself. He was tremendously sorry to see tears in those beautiful eyes. His heart was shattered.

"Perhaps this wretched vagabond is not worthy of your love, my dear Princess," he said dejectedly.

This time she stretched her hand out to keep it on his mouth. "Don't say such nonsense again." Her voice was tender but firm. "I love you and will continue to love you till my death. It was you for whom I seem to have waited all these years. I'll keep waiting for you, till you return from your search." She said, with tears in her eyes and took her hand off his mouth.

Dev was moved. He stared at her with many streams of love, gratitude, wonder and admiration running in his heart. Kneeling down before her, he took her hands in his, touched them with his closed eyes and kissed them. Her hands seemed to have melted in his. "Dev is yours forever, my sweet Princess;" He said. His voice was deep. "The prisoner of your heart will never go anywhere without your consent. I'll stay back if you command me, my Princess."

His touch was as delicate as the snowflakes falling in the winter, and as warm as the sunshine in the early morning. Lila trembled at the touch. She gazed in his eyes and felt lost in them. There was such tenderness, such affection and love in those deep eyes. Her heart felt like melting.

"I never want you to feel forced into marriage, Dev. Even though I know how I feel about you only in these few days, I would rather wait. Where do you want to go?" she asked softly, presently recovering her composure.

"I came to this city wishing to study with the Sage Ramanam, you know. He seems to be the person who can assuage my doubt and restore my self-worth."

"When do you wish to go to him?"

"I will go to him, only if you allow me to go." He said earnestly gazing at her eyes.

A drop of tear, pure and pristine like the morning dew, fell from her eyes.

"I'll not restrict you, Dev. My love knows to give freedom to the beloved, and it knows to wait," she said as calmly as she could manage.

"You are amazing, Lila." He softly said gazing at her. Her calm love and silent dignity was making him more weak and vulnerable in limitless love and gratitude. Lila softly pressed her hands against his, saying nothing.

"I'm and will be eternally grateful to you." He whispered again.

At this, she smiled; her tearful smile sparkled in the moonlight. His heart tore at the sight. The more he knew her, the more deeply he came to love and admire her. She was the one, the only one with whom he felt such oneness of heart in his whole life.

She was the one who gave him the taste of freedom even within the bond of her intense love. He was feeling blessed to experience such an amazing love. The thought of parting from her was tearing his heart, though. They sat together silently till late in the evening.

The King and his Prime Minister came late. From a distance they saw them sitting silently together. The King was surprised, and a secret happiness ran through his heart. "Won't they make a good match, Shyam?" he whispered to his friend. Shyam was surprised too, finding them sitting so close to each other.

"Sure! Dev is a boy one among millions, no doubt," he said thoughtfully, "though we know nothing about his family."

"I have full trust over Lila's choice and prudence," said the King, "I won't bother about his whereabouts, if she happens to choose him."

"True." said Shyam, "Besides I have seen the boy closely. He is a person of exceptional integrity."

"And didn't we see his ready wit, courage and noble spirit today? That surely speaks on his behalf," said the King, enthused.

"Right. Over and above that, he has the gift of his music, a kind heart and erudition." Shyam nodded. "I am sure, if anybody could make Princess Lila happy, it would be him."

When they arrived where the two were seated, Dev stood up and respectfully bowed, greeting the King and his friend.

"Sorry guys, even today we are late," said the King. He and his Prime Minister sat on a couch nearby.

"Are the royal emissaries of Panda still here?" asked Lila.

"Yes, my dear", said the King, "They'll be leaving tomorrow."

"We were busy discussing on a common project regarding the distribution of the waters of the Ganges, you know." Shyam said to Dev.

"I see; that's great," Dev said politely.

"Forget it, for now." said the King, brushing the topic aside. "Now I wish to listen to the flute. It will be relaxing after such a hectic day. Will you please play it for us, Dev?"

"With pleasure, Your Majesty," Dev said courteously. He took his seat on a piece of rock nearby and took his flute to his lips. The music covered the valley with its gorgeous silky wings and flied to the mountains.

When Dev was playing his flute immersed within him, Lila was struggling hard to resist her tears.

'Why do you let him go?' Something kept whispering inside her. 'Keep him from going; bind him fast with the soft fetters of your love.'—

She felt a drop of tear rolling down her cheeks before she realized she was openly crying. Swiftly she wiped it off with the back of her hand and looked around to be sure that nobody noticed it. She pretended to listen to the music with rapt attention.

She had thought it over. Unless his inner urge of finding his self identity was fulfilled, he would remain but a shadow of what he really was born to be— a gigantic tree giving shelter to many. Her prudence could see through his magnificent potential. No. She won't keep him from going. She couldn't endure seeing him helplessly submitting himself to a mediocre life. She would like to let him go instead, following his calling. She would like to see him fulfilled...

With these thoughts tears came in streams, which she could not contain, in spite of her effort. Drops after drops kept falling down her cheeks, unnoticed by all.

Dev finished playing his flute taking everybody in its spell. It was late in the evening when they took leave from the King and the Princess.

The King turned to his daughter, after they departed. "This young man possesses exceptional talent and nobility. Doesn't he?" He said to her. Lila felt waves of tears choking her throat. She walked over to her father to sit beside him.

"Don't you like him, dear?" King asked her again. Unable to speak, she gently placed her head on her father's shoulder. The King affectionately patted over her head.

"I know, you like him," he said softly. "Who won't like such a man? He possesses such a rare combination of goodness and intelligence, erudition and valor."

There was silence for a moment. "How about choosing him my successor to the throne? I'd be relieved to see you married to him." The King said again turning to her. "He would make an excellent King, after I leave the throne."

"No Papa, that's not possible; at least, not now." Lila said and sobbed, pressing her face hard against her father's shoulder.

"Why dear?" The King was bewildered; "Why not? Don't you like him?"

"It's not a question of my liking, Papa," she said after a pause; "I'd feel blessed to have him marry me."

"Then where's the problem?" The King asked impatiently.

"He's got an inner calling, Papa, which he must follow. He wishes to study with the revered Sage Ramanam."

"Doesn't he love you too?"

Lila silently nodded meaning to say 'yes', as tears came streaming down her face. Slowly, she collected herself and related Dev's story to her father.

The King listened to it all with patience. "I don't see any reason why he should be bothered about that." He said thoughtfully. "His Brahmin parents, who brought him up, are rightfully his parents; that's enough of his social identity. And when he marries you, he will belong to the royal family too. He doesn't need to find an identity elsewhere."

Lila shook her head.

"It's not a question of social recognition, Papa. He had enough of that when he was living in his village."

"Then what's it, dear?"

"It's a question of his feeling of self-worth. The story of his unknown birth has destroyed his self-pride of belonging to an erudite Brahmin lineage."

"This is strange!" The King blurted out.

"Only Brahmins are regarded worthy of having and imparting the knowledge of the Vedas, you know." She said calmly. "He feels his years of education and erudition has all been futile due to his unknown ancestry."

"He is unnecessarily making a simple thing complex. When he marries you nobody will ask what his vocation is."

"True, Papa. Not everybody feels like him."

"Why don't you persuade him to understand that?"

"No use, Papa." Lila said, a lump of tears forming in her throat. "I've tried, but the unfolding of his life has created a strange spiritual longing within him."

The King shrugged. He was perplexed. "I'll have a talk with him." He said, patting on her back. His heart became heavy, nevertheless. A frown appeared on his forehead.

They were walking together side by side. Neither of them spoke. Shyam was thinking about his friend's suggestion to get his daughter married to Dev. He was feeling happy and light-hearted at the thought. — There couldn't have been a better choice. Dev is just the perfect match for Princess Lila. This marriage will make everybody happy and at ease. This could prevent this bright and talented young man from pursuing his queer plan of studying with the sage Ramanam in the wilderness.

Dev was thinking of Lila. Never in his life has he felt such an intense attraction for any woman... Such emotions were unknown to him until he came to know her.

Suddenly he remembered Sania. Sania was beautiful too, but Dev never felt emotionally attached to her; he'd never been attracted to her. True; he used to be amused to listen to her constant chattering and enjoyed her friendly company. But this much is certain that he would never dream of sharing his life with her. She was like a cute little parrot. Dev felt sad to disappoint her love, though.

Lila took him breathless the moment he saw her. There is certainly something in her that is much more subtle and appealing than just her physical beauty, which is fascinating nevertheless.

Dev was wondering what it was that makes him breathless before her. Is it the subtle grace that envelops her persona? Is it the dignified silence that surrounds her? Or is it the pristine purity and profundity of her spirit?—

Dev was not quite sure what it was; but this was the thing that he was attracted to at the very first sight of her. He felt instantly drawn to her. Then her divine music swept him away. She is really unparalleled in her tenderness, beauty, intelligence and wisdom. –

His whole being fervently desired to be near her. So strong and irresistible was her pull, Dev felt like going back to her. He wished to tell her that he had abandoned his plan to leave. How happy she would be! Dev could do anything to see her happy. A deep sigh came out of him. He stopped for a moment.

Shyam walked a few steps forward and turned to him.

"What happened?"

"Nothing…!" Dev sighed and caught up with him.

He felt scattered and divided in his mind. The strange ache in his heart was consuming him. He was torn apart by two different pulls, both as powerful as the currents of the overflowing Mountain Rivers in the monsoon. He was feeling tired and exhausted.

But somehow he knew that in his present state of mind he couldn't make her truly happy. The initial passion will soon wear away to give way to frustration and disappointment, because he would be unable to offer her his whole being and his whole mind which she truly deserves. He'd be scared to make his soul bare to her… so utterly empty and worthless it felt. Such a fragmented state of mind can neither bring him fulfillment nor would it allow him to fulfill her. A deep sigh came out of him.

They walked into the large dining hall to have their dinner. They were met with the smell of freshly baked bread and lamb curry. Shyam noticed Dev engrossed within himself. He took his seat and looked up. "Princess Lila seems to have a liking for you, Dev." He said with a smile.

"Yes." Dev said without a hesitation.   Shyam was surprised at his candid reply. They were seated face to face on the dining table.

"Yes?" Shyam lifted his eyebrow.

"Yes," said Dev."We love each other, my esteemed friend." He softly added.

Shyam was surprised and delighted.

"The King's guess is right then." He said smiling, "He was saying you two would make a good match."

"Did they finish building the hut on the mountain?" He abruptly changed the topic.

Shyam was taken aback at this sudden turn. "It's about to be completed in a couple of days", he said, puzzled, "but, are you still thinking of leaving for the mountain?"

"Yes, Sir", he said briefly.

"Are you serious?" Shyam sounded grave. "I thought you abandoned that crazy idea."

Dev looked at him and nodded. "It's not possible…"

"What's not possible?"

The cook and attendants came to serve the food. Dev waited till they left.

"Abandoning the thought of leaving for the mountain…" He said catching the thread of their conversation.

"Didn't you say that you two love each other?"

"Yes, I did." Dev said faintly. "But I didn't say that I abandoned my plan to study."

"Don't be in a hurry to take a decision that you might have to repent, Dev…" Shyam sounded anxious and annoyed. "King Vikram is very hopeful about you. He would like you to marry the Princess and settle here."

Dev looked up at him. This was the toughest decision of his life. Was he going to ruin the happiness of these people only to satisfy his selfish whim? No; he never meant to do so. Only the things turned in such a manner that now the search for his self-identity seems to clash with their happiness. What can he possibly do? –

"I am grateful to the King for the trust and confidence he placed on me." Dev said earnestly, "And I'll always remain immensely grateful to you, my friend, for the love and affection you showered on a stranger like me." He paused for a few moments, as if, to collect and organize his thoughts.

"And what about Princess Lila?" Shyam said impatiently, "Say you are grateful to her for her love!" His last words sounded sarcastic.

"Indeed I am!" Dev said, ignoring the sarcasm in Shyam's tone. "Her love has enriched my life beyond imagination. I am eternally grateful to her. Had she not given me her permission, I couldn't have pursued my plan to study." He lowered his head to hide his emotion.

Shyam was observing Dev quietly. He could see the inner struggle the boy was going through, but he couldn't quite get the reason of his hesitation.

"Being grateful is not enough, Dev…" He said in a somber voice. Dev lifted his head to say something. Shyam raised his hand to stop him.

He looked worried and frustrated. "Though we know nothing about your family, Dev, you are no longer a stranger to us." Shyam said again. "In these few days you have won our hearts in your own merit. But you have no right to let us down with such an irresponsible move. I entreat you to not break the hearts of those that loved and trusted you." He said again.

"But I didn't…" Dev tried to say something feebly, but could not finish.

Shyam interrupted. "Don't act irresponsibly, Dev" he said. "Did Lila happily give you her consent?"

Dev shook his head in despair. "She was very sad to let me go. She said she'll forever wait for me." He said sadly. "Her patience and piety is making me weak from inside, you know. That's the reason I wish to leave as early as possible."

"But what's the urgency Dev? Why must you go?" Shyam asked in despair.

Dev stared at him for a moment.

"The urgency is in my heart; it's very difficult to explain, my friend." He said.

Shyam was not convinced. This is sheer willfulness and recklessness of the youth. He doesn't know the implication of what he is going to do. Shyam must do something about it. This young man is going to take a wrong decision that would mar the happiness of the Royal family. He must be prevented from doing this.

— "Look; Princess Lila is no ordinary woman, you know." Shyam said mildly chiding him. "You should consider yourself fortunate that you won her heart. Your reckless decision can ruin not only your life, but also hers. Can't you see…?"

"I know…" Dev muttered. "But I really don't see a way out…"

"No more excuse, Dev." There was authority in Shyam's voice. "I'm sure you are mature enough to see that you can have everything here — everything one can wish in life —

love, comfort, wealth, luxury, power and social recognition; we can even arrange wise scholars for you to study right here in the Palace. You don't need to go elsewhere for that!" Shyam tried to persuade the boy.

Dev was quietly listening. A sad smile crossed his face.

"Lila is one in a million, I know. I do think myself fortunate to have her in my life and my heart breaks thinking of having to go away from her." He said, "But, for the other things you've mentioned, I'm sorry to disappoint you, my esteemed friend, they are meaningless to me in the present context."

Shyam looked very dejected. Worry and distress was written on his face. Dev felt very sorry at the distress of this kind friend. He felt very bad about being the cause of distress for these people, who unquestioningly trusted him and showered their love and affection upon him.

"I have already told Lila. I'll tell you today what makes me compelled to take such a decision." He said again.

Shyam became very quiet and silently stared at him. Dev hated to recite the weird story of his life again. But he had no other option. Shyam listened to him with patience. After he finished telling his story, Dev noticed a change in his facial expression.

"I admire your integrity, Dev," He said, "— the integrity that did not allow you to live a life of pretense. Your character and integrity itself give you an identity that is rare and unique."

"I am grateful to you for your understanding, Sir. You have been kind and affectionate toward me as ever." Dev said. "But I cannot possibly explain, Sir, what is going on within me, from the day I knew that I was born of unknown parents, of unknown ancestry; I have been shaken to the core of my being. I lost my sense of belonging and self-pride."

He paused to catch with his breath.

"I can no longer depend on any worldly identity; I can no longer depend on anything that can be snatched away in a moment." He said in deep anguish. "I've abandoned my home to find my identity— an identity that will give me a sense of self-worth. I'll remain unfulfilled and restless, before I can find that." He sighed.

Shyam listened to him. His heart was filled with silent compassion for this youth.

Dev was feeling somewhat relieved to be able to speak out his mind. He kept quiet for a few moments, and then he spoke again. "Lila is exceptionally understanding, you know; she understands my pain; she understands the longing of my heart; but that makes me all the more vulnerable... You know what? My mind is often tempting me to abandon my search and stay back here to be with her. I love her very deeply... I love her from the bottom of my heart." His voice choked.

"Why don't you listen to your heart, Dev?" Shyam said kindly. "Why don't you stay back?"

"I've thought about that; but my mind is scattered and fragmented. It's beyond my control." Dev said in frustration. "In such a state of mind how can I possibly make her happy? I can't." He said with a sigh.

Shyam sighed too. He had thought it over. Perhaps, Dev was right. The boy needs some time to adapt to the strange reality of his life. Practicing under the guidance of the wise sage might help him do just that. The company of the wise man might help him recover from his anguish and accept life as it is.

"You are probably right, Dev." He said openly. "If you are not at peace with yourself, you can't make anybody happy." Both were silent for a while. Shyam looked grave and thoughtful.

"Go, if you must;" He said again, "but take the suggestion of this old friend, my boy. Life is too precious to squander it away. Pursue your search with sincerity and intelligence, and once you feel that you are done with it, come back. We'll be eagerly waiting for you."

Dev looked up with gratitude in his eyes.

"I'll remember your advice, my esteemed friend." He said. "I feel grateful that destiny has blessed me with such a noble friend and mentor like you."

##

For the next couple of days Dev didn't visit the Palace. He kept himself shut inside his room. He felt stressed out. He was tremendously sorry for being the cause of distress to the persons who had unconditionally showered their love and affection upon him. He was feeling sorry for Lila, for

Shyam and for the King. They were suffering for no fault of them.

The hut was ready; he learnt from Shyam. It was like leaving the home for a second time. He was feeling so much connected to these people whom he did not know even a few weeks before. In the afternoon, Dev went to the royal garden.

Lila and Bella were sitting together in the garden. Bella found her friend lost in a deep melancholy mood. She was trying hard to know why Lila was not her usual self for the past few days. Just at that moment, her gaze fell on Dev coming their way toward the marble rock.

"Look my friend. Someone is coming," she whispered excitedly in her friend's ear as she gently nudged her. Surprised, Lila turned around and saw him coming; her heart stopped for a moment. Bella was astonished to notice the sudden change of the color on her face. Lila's face was radiant, beaming with a strange light. She blushed, but her gaze was fixed on his face.

After they were seated, Lila introduced Bella to him. He politely greeted Bella joining his palms to his chest.

Bella was impressed by his deep, rich voice and regal demeanor. There was something in him that made her admire this stranger. It was evident that Lila knew him intimately. Does she have a crush on him? Sure she has. With a man like Dev, it's easy for a woman to lose her head and her heart. Sensing that something was going on between them, Bella politely took leave and departed.

After Bella departed, Lila gazed fully at his eyes. He too was gazing at hers. The depth of her shining black eyes gave him a heart-stopping joy. Dev felt he was losing himself in the oceanic depth of those eyes. For a long while neither of them spoke a word. Finally, he softly uttered her name.

At this her eyes were filled with tears; her ears were thirsting to hear the dear voice she was apprehensive of losing. Dev walked over to sit by her side. He took her hands and mildly caressed them. "Lila, my sweetheart, please forgive this reprobate of yours." He said in a deep voice.

Lump of tears choked her throat. Unable to speak, she gently pressed her soft hands in to his, and tears came streaming down her face. A sea of feelings stirred Dev from inside. He sat motionless like a statue, not knowing how to console her.

After a few moments, she collected herself. A strange serenity and poise shone on her face.

"Do you see the snowy Himalaya, Dear?" She said with a sigh. "And look at the blue beyond that. It is so near the mountain and so far away from it as well. Our lives are like them."

Dev was stirred. "Please don't say such a thing, sweetheart." He whispered. "I won't go there if it gives you so much pain. Nothing is more important to me than your happiness."

She shook her head in desperation. "No, no, no — darling...!" Her voice choked. She bit her lip and cleared her throat. "Sacrificing your happiness for my sake would only make me unhappier. Don't do that, please. I want to see you happy and fulfilled."

Dev was overwhelmed. He was struggling hard within him to control the emotions storming within.

She collected herself again and a calm smile shone on her tearful face. "You came to take leave from me; right?"

Dev lowered his head; his voice choked. The pain of imminent parting was tearing his heart.

"Go, my love. Go in peace." She said again. "I pray your search be fruitful and rewarding. And when you are fulfilled, come back to me, to be my teacher, my lover, my lord and my friend in this life." She said in an unruffled tone.

"I love you, darling. I love you with all my heart…" His voice broke. He was amazed at her serene reaction.

She turned from him and gazed over the mountain to conceal her tears. Dev sat motionless by her side, his feelings numbed.

After a while, she looked at him again and her eyes melted upon him in a strange tenderness. Dev kept looking at that dear face with deep love, affection and adoration. He was struggling against him. His mind rebelled. Part of his mind didn't want to go away from her. Gazing steadily upon him, she smiled with tears in her eyes. Her tearful smile disconcerted him more.

Evening was slowly approaching, stealing the light of the day. The somber shadow of the tall oaks and pines made the garden darker. Burying his tears within his heart he stood up to take leave from her before her tears made him too weak to leave.

She stood staring at his departing form. "Go my love; but you can't go far. The bond of my love will draw you here." She whispered to herself. "It is stronger than you can imagine. I know you'll come back to me."

The evening breeze whipped through her hair, swelling the growing chill in her heart. The garden felt cold and vacant and the memory of those happy moments already felt as an event of lifetime ago.

Leaving Home Again

As he walked away from her, a strange sense of loneliness came over him. It felt as if he were far, far away from everyone in the world he had ever known. He felt completely lost and alone in his world.

He was feeling tired and exhausted; however he must meet the King, before he leave. The gatekeeper saluted him as he entered the room. King Vikram was sitting alone in his room on a couch. He looked heartbroken. Dev bowed to the King. The King looked up to him with a vacant expression in his eyes.

"I have come to take leave from you, your Majesty; please give me your permission." Dev mumbled.

The King stared at him for a while. "Did you take leave from Lila?" He asked.

Dev silently nodded to say 'yes'.

"Why must you go, Dev? Couldn't you stay among us, being one of us?" the King implored, his voice full of sadness. "As an unhappy father, I would have begged from you the happiness of my daughter, if that kept you from leaving us…"

Dev remained silent. He felt all his feelings numbed and he did not find words.

"You mustn't go, Dev" the King said in desperation grabbing his hands. "You shall not, I tell you."

Dev didn't know how to reciprocate to this loving request. It numbed him more. Like a stone statue he stood silently feeling guilty of an unknown offense. His head stooped.

"I might have forced you to stay with us, if she herself hadn't given you permission to go." The King finally let go of his hands. "Silly girl… What does she know of the world? Why did she happen to love such a brute like you?" The King's voice broke.

Dev was feeling terribly sorry and guilty, for the offence he unwillingly committed by winning their hearts. He could feel the despair and worry of a father. But he couldn't say anything.

"Life on the mountain is not for you, Dev." The King said again, coaxing him. "One who has won the heart of my daughter should live in Palace and rule the kingdom."

"I feel terribly sorry, Your Majesty, for disappointing all of you. Please forgive me, if you can."

"I wish I could find a good reason to send you to the prison."

"I submit myself to you for imposing on me whatever punishment you deem fit for me."

The King shook his head dejectedly. "It's our misfortune, Dev that we couldn't keep you from going." The King said again, "Go where you wish, but, we'll certainly wait for you to come back to us."

"I'll be ever grateful to you, Your Majesty, for understanding my compulsion, which makes me incapable of keeping the honor of your words." He benignly said. "I feel terribly sorry about that. Nobody on earth knows better than me how I yarn to come back to my beloved as soon as my doubts are assuaged. I'll remember your words." Dev bowed low to him and left.

It was late in the evening when Dev came back from the Palace. He was feeling awfully exhausted and stressed out. He found Shyam busy in instructing the servants to make the carriage ready for the next morning. He also found tins of foods and other utilities gathered.

He took Shyam aside and asked him what this was all about. "We'll be leaving early in the morning, tomorrow." He said."These should be ready today."

Dev was taken aback. "What do you mean?" he said, amazed. "I don't need all this. I'll be leaving all alone and I wish to go by foot."

At his obstinate request, Shyam left the idea of making the provisions for food for him; but he insisted to accompany Dev to the mountain in his carriage.

"Please allow me to accompany you, my young friend," he said, "and allow me to visit you from time to time." After much resisting, Dev yielded to his request on condition that Shyam might visit him once in a while and only with the usual offering he used to make to the sage. Shyam agreed. For a reason unknown to him, he felt deeply affectionate to this valiant youth.

Life on the Mountain

They climbed the mountain silently on the narrow trail, walking and resting together. Dev carried his bag with his meager possession of a few cloths, a cotton towel and his flute. Shyam carried with him some earthen lamps, clarified butter, sweets, dates and nuts.

After a while they reached the lake on the mountain. They found the small, tidy hut built on the lakeside near the cave. The sage could not be seen around.

Together they entered the hut. They found a wooden cot near the window, with a pillow, rugs and a mat on it; there was a fire-place in one corner and an earthen stove and some utensils on another side.

Dev knew these arrangements had been made at the direction of Shyam. He was feeling deeply grateful to him. Shyam walked over to the wooden shelf and kept the bundle of earthen lamps, butter, dates and nuts on it.

"This will come handy while you adjust in your new life, Dev." He said, smiling. Somehow he was feeling perturbed inside to think about the inconveniences Dev must endure in this austere life he had chosen for himself.

Before Dev could say anything, he turned to Dev and held his hands, shaking them gently. "Take good care of you, my young friend." He said, earnestly.

"Yes, I will. Thank you." Dev said softly. "Thank you, my friend, for taking so much care to see to my comfort on this mountain." He said again.

They approached the cave looking for the sage. Seeing them coming his way, the sage came out of the cave. Both of them greeted him bowing low.

"So, you have come!" He said, winking; Dev bowed down to touch his feet and smiled silently.

"Did you bring the food with you?" The old man asked.

Shyam offered the sweets to him.

"No, no, no. Not this. I am not asking for me. What will he have for his midday meal?" he enquired pointing to Dev.

"My friend has kept some fruits and nuts for me, there in my hut, Sir." Dev said."From tomorrow onwards I'll find the fruits and roots, seeds and nuts that are available here on the mountain."

The sage shook his head. "That'll not do. You cannot survive, young man, on the meager meal that I am used to." He said to Dev. Turning to Shyam he said, "Please send your men tomorrow with a ration of rice, lentils, potato, dried beans, salt, Ghee and black pepper, sufficient for him to sustain for a month. And please send your men once a month to supply this ration for him as long as he is here."

The old man tuned to Dev again. "You will boil rice, lentils, beans and potato for yourself. With Ghee, salt and pepper, they'll not taste bad." The sage grinned.

Shyam was very happy at this arrangement and Dev was feeling embarrassed at this special arrangement for him. However, considering the practical aspect of things, he relented.

Late in the morning, Shyam took leave from the sage and Dev accompanied him down to the foot of the hill, where the horse-carriage was waiting for him.

"Please take care of your health." Dev said as they reached the carriage. Shyam was overwhelmed. "I think I'll… we'll miss you, Dev," he said.

"I'll miss you too, my friend," Dev said softly.

"Do you want me to say something to the Princess for you?"

Dev looked down and shook his head, intending to say 'no.'

After the driver took the carriage away, Dev turned to the narrow forest path and climbed up the mountain trail to return to the cave. This was the beginning of a new life for him.

Bella was sitting on a couch in the large living room. She was waiting for Shyam. Just a while ago, she visited the Princess. She looked sad and forlorn. Her disheveled hair, unadorned look and dejected countenance were evidently telling that something went wrong with her. Her faraway gaze was fixed toward the snowy peaks of the Himalaya. Somehow they reminded her of Dev and her eyes were full of tears. Bella was observing her silently.

"You are in love with him, aren't you?" Bella whispered. Lila smiled with tears in her eyes.

"It was silly of me not to guess that you could have a crush on that stranger, honey..." Bella said. "You should have told me this."

"His name is Dev." Lila said softly, again with a tearful smile.

"Hmmm. You introduced him to me the other day. He really looks like a Prince."

"Does he love you too?" she asked again.

At this Lila nodded to say 'yes', and sobbed, covering her face in her palms.

Bella was perturbed to see her tears. "Won't you tell me what happened?" she said earnestly gazing at her.

Lila looked up to her. Her eyes had a reddish tinge. She mildly grabbed the hands of her friend. "Sure, I'll tell you, Bella. To whom else can I unburden my heart?" She said, as she hugged her.

She told her everything from the day she met Dev. Reliving the story, sometimes her face became bright like the full moon and the next moment a sad veil covered it.

Bella silently listened to it all. This was so crazy of her. She thought. "Why did you let him go, Lila?" Bella asked after a while. "You shouldn't have."

"I allowed him to go because he trusted the decision on me, Bella." Lila said sadly.

"This is strange, my friend! You let him go and now you are crying."

"You know, he said he won't go, if I did not permit."

"So what?" Bella was perplexed. "You should have prevented him from going."

"No; I couldn't do that." Lila said sobbing in despair, "He said my happiness was more important to him than anything else."

"So...?" Bella frowned. She couldn't see why this silly girl permitted her lover to go.

Lila remained silent for a while. Tears filled her eyes again. "How could I not let him go, Bella, knowing in my heart that he was prepared to sacrifice everything for my sake, even his sense of worth...?"

"If I didn't allow him to go, he would submit to living an ordinary life here even if he would be humiliated and tormented by his soul every moment of his life— all for the sake of my happiness. How could I do that?" she said again, regaining her composure.

"Noble and sublime is your love, dear," Bella said softly. "I can't even imagine of making such a sacrifice."

"You know what? If I had not permitted him to go for his search, he would have remained unfulfilled and scattered for his whole life." Lila said with a heavy sigh. "He would have remained with me like a great Banyan tree pruned and planted in a small tub. I couldn't bear that."

Bella nodded. "Perhaps, you are right, Lila. But how'll you survive for the rest of your life, in case he never returns?"

"I don't know, Bella." The Princess sobbed again. "Can you please go to the house of uncle Shyam, and bring me his news?" She begged.

The request of her friend has made Bella come to Prime Minister's residence. Presently she heard noises outside the portico. Probably the carriage returned. Shyam entered the hallway and saw Bella sitting in the living room.

As he entered the room, Bella made a bow and greeted him with a sad smile.

"Uncle, did you leave Dev, there on the mountain?" she said. "The Princess is eager to know his whereabouts, you know."

"Yes. I know," Shyam said with a sigh. He was feeling unhappy and dejected as he returned from the mountain. He was terribly missing Dev. Though unequal in age and status, somehow they grew very friendly and caring toward each other in this short period.

"Please ask her not to worry about him. The sage will take good care of him and I'll visit him from time to time." He said in consolation.

After Bella left with the news, Shyam left for the court. His heart was heavy. He didn't feel like having his lunch.

The Secret Wisdom

Dev found the sage sitting on a mat in front of his cave. He walked over to him and took his seat near him. The sage looked up. "Now tell me why you came here." He said, winking.

"You know it, revered Sir; right?" Dev humbly said.

"I may know everything about you, Dev," the sage said gently, gazing far toward the forest of Pines, "but it won't help you clear your doubt and remove the restlessness from your mind."

"I came here to find my self-identity, Sir," Dev said politely. "Please be my teacher and show me the way."

"I accept you as my disciple, Dev." The sage smiled.

Dev has heard that the sage has the knowledge of past, present and future. He was curious to know if that was true. "Can you tell me, Master, who my real parents are?" He asked benignly.

"It is possible to know that, if you are interested." The sage became somber. "But I'll advise you to direct your effort to a far greater purpose. Know your real self. That would be much more fulfilling for you and then such other trivial knowledge may come just as a by-product."

"How can I know my real self?"

"You will know your real self, Dev, through the practice of meditation," the sage said kindly.

"Does a self really exist?" asked Dev.

"Who's asking the question, Dev," the sage said, joking, "If a self doesn't exist?"

"Yes, but, I mean....you know...." Dev scratched his head to find the appropriate words. His question sounded silly, he knew. But his head was crowded with all these information of 'self', 'super-Self' and 'no-self'— the information he gathered from his years of study of the holy books.

The sage took pity on him. "Okay; first tell me, what is a self? What do you normally mean by the word?" He said again.

"Well... It is my existence," said Dev.

"And what is your existence made of? It is made of your body, your thoughts and your emotions; right?" the sage said, smiling.

"Right," Dev said, "but I know they don't remain the same all the time. Do they?"

"Exactly that was my point, Dev." The sage said, "The self you know as 'you' is always changing. If you observe your mind, you will find that your thoughts and emotions are continuously changing. The cells in your body are dying too every moment to be replaced by new cells."

"True." Dev was listening to the old man intently, trying to grasp every word he spoke.

"But did you ever ask yourself who knows this change?" The sage said again, startling him.

"No, Sir, I didn't." Dev muttered uncertainly. –

For the first time in his life he was being aware that the dying cells in his body could not possibly know the nature of the new cells arriving to replace them. A dying thought cannot possibly know which thought is going to come the next moment. Then who is going on witnessing these changing phenomena of his body and mind?—

"There is a seer behind all these changing phenomena; this seer witnesses the changes." The sage said grinning at him. "If this witnessing presence was not there, who would ever know about the change? Do you get my point?"

"Sure!" Dev said, "Is this witnessing presence within me my real self?"

"You are very close to it", the sage smiled. "But only intellectual understanding will not do. Knowledge can liberate you only when you know it by experience. Unless you gain this knowledge as your own experience, those unreal shadow selves will dominate your mind beguiling you to take them as your identity."

"So true!" Dev nodded in agreement. He related to the sage the story of his strange life. "My old self, the young, accomplished Brahmin Dev died in my mind the moment I knew they were not my real parents." He said with a sigh. The sage was quietly listening to him.

"Revered teacher, does death happen in the mind, or in the body?" Dev asked again.

The sage was very happy with his question.

"You have understood it correctly. Death happens in the mind only." He said.

"You mean to say death is an illusion?"

"Yes!" A strange light was playing on the wrinkled countenance of the old man. "Death happens to the shadow selves only. Our shadow selves die many deaths, even in this life." The sage said.

This was a fantastic idea. But Dev couldn't disagree with what the sage said. He was absorbing the wisdom with all his being. He has seen the death of the shadow self of the arrogant Brahmin Dev; he has seen his old self replaced by his present self of a diffident, uncertain youth, who has no identity apart from the name 'Dev'.

And now the sage says that this self too will die one day. If it really be so, it will bring much relief. But then who will remain? He wondered.

"Revered Master, what does my real self look like? Does it have any resemblance with my body?" Dev spoke his thoughts aloud.

"The Self inhabits the body just as fragrance inhabits a flower, my son." The sage said, smiling. "It has no form. The Body is just a thought, an image, floating in our consciousness."The sage became silent.

Dev felt a subtle happiness running through his heart, though he could not grasp all of what the sage said. He was feeling happy and relieved to think that he didn't need to carry on the bundle of the worn out memory of his caste, clan, family and erudition. They gave him just a false shadow identity that never was his true self.

But doubt was still hovering in his mind. Though it all sounded good, Dev wanted get a strong foothold on the idea.

"But then who am I really? What my real witnessing self is made of?" He asked.

"Do not try to grasp it through your intellect, Dev." The sage mildly chided him; "It is impossible to grasp it that way…Okay, let me ask you, who knew about the death of your old self?" asked the sage.

"I knew," Dev said, perplexed.

"You're right." The sage said grinning. "But who is this 'I' that witnessed the death of proud and arrogant Dev?"

Dev shook his head. "I don't know."

"That's the correct attitude, my son, to begin your search." The said kindly. "Abide in this attitude of not-knowing and seek to know who this I is. Go to the root of your "I" thought."

Dev was feeling good about the old man addressing him as 'son'. He was feeling more at ease with him.

"What is so special about my 'I', revered Sir? Doesn't everybody use this word when referring to themselves?"

"True. Everybody uses the word, Dev, but without knowing its secret." The sage whispered. "It is the source of all our power, knowledge and memory. It is the creative energy of God."

Dev was astounded to know this. He stared at his master in wide-eyed wonder.

"The 'I-consciousness' is what creates our world, Dev." The sage said again. "It is one with the essence of creative energy, which is also expressed by the sacred syllable 'Om'....O…O…O...M…M...M..."

The sage hummed the holy word, the word of words. It resounded in the valley. A shiver passed through Dev's spine. There was something in the utterance, a mysterious energy that reverberated through his whole being, stirring him from inside. The stillness of the forest was stirred too.

"It is the sound of silence..." the sage whispered, "It is the purest and the most basic vibration that exists at the root of all creation. Everything that you can see, touch, feel or perceive in this universe comes out of this divine vibration, my son.

Everywhere in this universe, you will find this vibration, Dev; it is there in the sound of your heart, in the functioning of your lungs and in the flow of the blood in your veins. Do you see it?" The sage blinked and closed his eyes for a while.

Dev was listening to him as if spellbound. All on a sudden, a light of clarity flashed through his mind brightening it up with a heretofore unknown clarity. He could feel the movement, the vibratory rhythm of life everywhere. He could see that there was this one Life, the vibratory energy, moving everything, breathing through every creature on earth!

He looked around to find this energy everywhere. Wherever he turned his gaze, everywhere he found this pure energy. He found it in the graceful glide of a bird, in the movement of a tiny worm crawling on the ground, in the branch of the trees swaying in the wind, in the setting Sun in the sky. He felt as if, everything was alive, vibrant and permeated by this vibratory energy, by this inner flowing essence.

Even the earth, rocks and pebbles seemed to be alive, breathing as he was breathing. Everything was made of pure Love. Dev closed his eyes to feel it. He found a strange golden egg, shimmering with a translucent golden light. What is it? He wondered. Suddenly an incomparable bliss filled his heart, which was hard to contain. His mind settled down after a while and resumed normal thinking.

The sage was intently observing Dev. "It is Shakti, the feminine energy, the motherly aspect of the Universe." He said, as if reading his mind.

"If Om is the motherly aspect of God, does God have a fatherly aspect too?"

"Yes, my son." The sage quipped. "We call that Shiva."

"Shiva?" Dev uttered in surprise. Shiva was a name of a god, he used to think.

"Yes," The sage was delighted to enlighten his disciple. "Shiva in reality is the silence of pure being, embodied. Om embraces this pure silence in its bosom, my son."

Both the master and the disciples remained silent for a while. Dev was enchanted by the mysterious wisdom he was receiving.

"Om is the sound of silence, Dev. It emerges from silence and merges in to the silence, you know." The sage said again, wishing to add more clarity to what he said earlier. "But this silence is not inert silence; it is self-aware and self illumined. By knowing it, you'll become established in the supremely peaceful unchanging `essence in the core of life."

Dev was listening to the sage with rapt attention. He was fascinated by what he was learning.

"Aren't you feeling hungry?" The sage changed the topic on a trice. An affectionate smile lit up his face. Suddenly Dev noticed that he was feeling very hungry indeed. He felt somewhat embarrassed to admit that, though. However, there was something in this old man, a mother-like quality, that made him feel very relaxed and at home with him.

"Yes, I am hungry." He candidly said, smiling. The sage went within his cave and came out with some chapattis, butter, honey and fruits within a bowl, and offered the bowl to Dev.

"The tribes of the neighboring village come to me from time to time, you know." He said, "They brought this food today, before you came."

Dev felt ashamed to share those offerings the villagers brought for his master. But the sage insisted.

"Don't worry. I take only one meal a day." he said.

Like a loving mother, the old man was sitting there, watching him as he ate, and insisting him to have more, until he was full. The sage showed him the clear mountain stream nearby. Dev washed his bowl and drank from it to his heart's content.

"You must be very tired today." The sage said. "Go to your hut and take rest. Come back to me when you're refreshed."

Dev bowed down to the sage and walked slowly back to his hut. He was already feeling light at his heart and a deep gratitude to this wise old man kept welling up within him.

The Master and the Disciple

He had a deep and refreshing sleep. When he woke up, it was dark. He could not make out what time it was. He looked out through his window. There was deep darkness outside. He was surprised that he slept so long. He came out of his hut and looked above at the waned moon. Its dim light was spread on the trees, grass, shrubs and on the lake, covering them in its veil of mysterious beauty. The night sky was studded with stars. There was deep palpable silence everywhere except for the occasional sound of the crickets.

Dev found the sage in a meditative mood, sitting on his mat. He walked over to him and took his seat at a distance, without saying a word. The sage did not seem to notice him. His eyes were half-closed. Dev was stunned by the peace and serenity reflected on his countenance. After a long while the sage opened his eyes and faintly smiled finding him there.

"Revered Master, will you please teach me how to meditate?" Dev said after a moment's hesitation.

"Yes, my son. I will," said the sage. His words were strong and calm.

"Meditation begins, Dev, with the enquiry 'Who am I?' Our 'I' thought holds the secret of our births and deaths." The sage said again in a kind voice.

"Did I have many births and many deaths?" asked Dev in innocent wonder.

"Yes, you had." He said, smiling. "There were millions of lives like the bubbles in an ocean, Dev!"

The old man was silent for a moment; Dev was listening to him spellbound. The air was still and not even a leaf was moving. As if the whole forest was listening to this noble wisdom in enthralling silence.

"Life moves in a circle, Dev; a circle of repetition, you know" The sage said again. "We repeat what we do everyday, eating, drinking, and sleeping; again the same thing, the next day. Birth after birth, we repeat the same mistakes, same experiences, the same cycle of enjoying pleasures and suffering the pains. And thus the story of birth and death goes on and on and on, until someday we break out of the circle; until we feel an inner urge to break open the cage of our limitation, to fly away in freedom to reach our infinite nature."

"How do we break away from our bondage?" Dev asked in wonder. He couldn't wait to know the secret.

The sage smiled. The innocence of a child and the prudence of a wise man were blended in his smile.

"We break away of our bondage, Dev, when we have a glimpse of our infinite nature." He said.

"Am I infinite?"

"You are infinite, Dev. We are indeed the Universe expressing itself as you and I."

"Why don't we understand that, revered Sir?"

"It is because of our identification with our body, which our senses report as finite. This identification creates the bondage."

"Don't our senses give us a correct picture of the reality?"

"No." The sage quipped.

"Am I not my body?" Dev wondered aloud.

"No, my son." The sage continued, "Your Body is a just a thought floating in your consciousness. We are the consciousness itself."

Dev felt as if a beam of light passing through him which lighted his heart for a moment. "If the body is merely a thought, revered Master, all of these lives, the births and deaths happen in the thoughts only!" he said, astonished.

"You are right." The sage glanced at him with a kind smile. "They are all imaginations floating in the consciousness, just like dreams."

Dev was fascinated by this insight. "Our 'I am' thought is the unchanging curtain on which the changing panorama of our births and deaths appears and disappears." The sage said again.

The sage taught Dev to meditate on his "I" thought. He taught him to meditate on his breath.

"Breath is the first manifestation of your 'I' thought, my son," he said. "The breath contains the sacred life-force. By meditating on it, you will go beyond thoughts. And when your mind quiets down you experience your eternal self as an inner sense of peace, joy and well-being."

Dev felt a pleasant and warm sensation rising along his spine. He felt like becoming lighter than a floating white cloud. His heart danced in joy. He knew in his heart that this on-the-top-of-the-world feeling appeared due to the pure energy he just received from his master. He had heard of it before. This is called Shaktipat initiation, by which an enlightened master transfers his energy to his disciple. It was for the second time that he had such an experience today.

"I am grateful to you, my revered Master," he said. "Thank you for teaching me the way."

The old man smiled in the moonlight. His smile was as tender and nourishing as the moonlight. It gladdened Dev's heart and touched it. He was full of gratitude to receive the secret knowledge that would enable him to look beyond his mundane existence.

The sage, as if, read his mind. "There is no such thing as mundane, my boy." he said with a kind smile lighting up his face again. "Everything is sacred; everything is the auspicious Om, the supreme reality. As you progress on the path, you will see it for yourself."

Dev was silent. This old man was amazing, he thought in admiration. He was enthralled by what he was experiencing. He could plainly see that this old man had the power to transmit his experience and wisdom. He would like to be with him forever to learn the eternal secret of this existence; he thought. He could do anything to repeat this euphoric experience he had just had.

The sage seemed to read his mind again and changed the topic in an instant.

"What will you have for your supper?" he said. "Go within my cave and bring out whatever is left." Dev quietly obeyed the sage. There were chapattis, molasses and ghee, more than enough for one man to eat.

"Take them with you," said the sage with a grin. "Consume whatever you can, and if something is left, you may use it up in the morning."

Dev felt obliged at the kindness and affection of this old man. But he hesitated. What will he have for his meal tomorrow?

The old man knew what was going on in his mind. "Don't worry for me, young man," he said. "I am used to forego a meal or two, without any difficulty."

Seeing that Dev was not convinced with what he said, the old man spoke up again. "Every alternative day the woodcutters and honey gatherers come to me from the village at the other side of this mountain. They use to bring some food for me."

Dev was astonished and ashamed at his folly of not allowing Shyam to bring the cereals and grains, which he planned to bring along.

"How long are you sustaining yourself, Sir, in this way, with such a meager meal?" Dev wondered aloud.

"Ninety Years." The sage blinked at him.

Dev was about to drop the bowl of food in astonishment. He thought that the sage was around seventy something.

"Ninety years!" He gasped. "How old are you then?"

The sage laughed. "I came here on this mountain when I was about your age."

Dev's confusion turned to bewilderment, and in amazed disbelief he stared at the sage. The man looked at least forty years younger than his age.

The sage was amused at his wonder. "I am over hundred and ten." He said again. "I'll teach you the technique to defeat aging. Now go and take your meal."

"This is much more than I can consume alone," Dev said in weak protest. But the sage persuaded him to take the bowl with him. Dev was overwhelmed at his kindness.

After he finished his meal, Dev washed the bowl, and sat silently on a big stone beside the stream. The night air was heavy with the scent of an unknown flower.

As the silent hours of the night passed, the forest on the mountain became more and more silent. Dev was feeling enchanted. The words of the sage were still ringing in his ears. He sat on the lotus pose beneath a tall tree and centered his attention on his breath. Within a few moments, he became absorbed in meditation. He meditated till late in the night, until the moon tilted over to the west.

The next morning, he woke up at the sweet chirping of the birds. After washing in the stream and taking his bath in its cooling flow, Dev sat down to meditate. When he rose from his seat, he heard men talking at a distance.

Surprised, he peeped through his window to find two men carrying bundles at their head coming toward his hut.

They came to him, put the bundles down on the ground and bowed low before him. Shyam had sent them. Dev gave them some sweet to eat and they departed.

Dev opened up the bundles. There were rice, lentils, potato, salt, sugar, pepper, honey, ghee, raisins, dates, dried beans and nuts nicely packed. He also found some raw vegetables. Dev was charmed at his friend's caring attention to the detail. He walked over to his Master.

"Revered Master, I beg to cook the meal for you today." He said, "My friend has sent the grocery."

"Have you ever cooked a meal?" the sage asked with a grin.

"No, revered Sir; but it's easy!" He smiled. "Back in our home I have seen my momma cooking meals for us."

"Okay." The sage said with a glimmer in his eyes. "I accept your invitation today. From tomorrow onwards, you will cook only for yourself. I'll manage as usual."

"No, Master," Dev humbly refuted, "Please! Once in a day we'll share our food together." He begged this of his teacher to prevent the sage going without a meal, in case the village folks failed to bring the food some day.

The sage stared on his face as if to read his thoughts and relented to his request with a smile and an affectionate pat on his back.

But cooking in the forest was not as easy as Dev thought it would be. His inexperience showed in everything he did. He collected some raw twigs and tried to make a fire in his earthen stove. The smoke irritated his eyes to tears and almost blinded his sight as he tried to make a fire from them.

Ultimately when he was successful in lighting a fire bringing in some dry twigs, he could not decide how much water to boil so the rice would be boiled right. After he put the water to boil, he cut some vegetables, and along with the lentils he put them all in the pot of boiling rice. Finally, he poured some ghee within the boiling mixture. The nice aroma of the ghee spread around.

A complacent smile appeared on his face to think that he had done it all. He could now relax and wait for the food getting ready; he thought. But just a while later his smile disappeared to find that water dried in the saucepan and the rice was only half boiled. God! How much water was needed to make the rice soft and eatable?

He hurriedly went out to bring the water from the stream. By the time he was back with the bucket of water, he found the fire about to go out. He lit a fire again.

Finally, when he was finished with his cooking, Dev was feeling miserable staring at the food. The rice formed in to a lump. He was thinking whether he could swallow the thing himself; he could not imagine of offering it to his teacher. He was praying that the old man won't come for his lunch. But at the noontime the sage came. Dev hurriedly offered him a seat.

"I don't think you would be able to eat what I have cooked." He said in an apologetic tone.

There was a twinkle of amusement in the eyes of the old man. "I am hungry," he said, "give me whatever you have cooked."

Dev was embarrassed beyond limit. He offered him a chunk on a platter.

"Where is yours?" asked the sage.

He made Dev take his share of the food and both of them sat down to eat.

With the corner of his eyes Dev looked cautiously at his teacher to guess his irritation to taste this uneatable thing. But to his amazement he found the sage eating the food with obvious delight. This made him feel somewhat relieved. He took a bite of the food, realizing that he had forgotten to add salt to it. He secretly looked at his Master again to gauge his reaction but he found absolutely no trace of complain there. The old man was eating mindfully with obvious satisfaction.

"Do you need some salt?" Dev said gaining some courage, "I think I have forgotten to add salt to it."

The sage looked up and smiled. "No, my son; you are a good cook" he said sincerely, "I liked the food."

Dev was taken aback at these words of appreciation and a feeling of joy ran through his chest that helped him to gulp the food down his throat. He would learn to cook better for the sake of this amazing old man; he silently promised to himself. He started to love his master, who had a wealth of compassion, love and wisdom, greater than any mortal he had ever seen.

In the afternoon, Dev found the sage sitting on a rug in front of his cave. He silently sat down nearby. The sage seemed indrawn within himself. His eyes were half-closed. Dev didn't feel like talking. Suddenly He felt an urge to meditate. Dev sat in an upright posture and closed his eyes. He did not know how long he meditated. A surge of profound peace swept him and he felt like dissolving in an ocean of white light that took him in its embrace to melt him in it.

The feeling of deep peace lingered within him even after he rose from his seat of meditation. The sage was sitting reclined on a rock with his eyes closed. Dev knew in his heart that by the grace of the sage, he just had a glimpse of the exalted state, in which the sage naturally abides. With deep reverence, he made a bow to his master and departed.

The Forest Ascetic

Dev took a little while to adjust to his life on the mountain. He learnt to make a reserve of dry woods and twigs for lighting a fire. He learnt to wash his clothes in the water of the lake. He learnt to cook a wholesome meal with the rice, lentils, beans and potatoes.

He loved to take his bath in the in the clear water of a waterfall and he took delight in watching flocks of swan flying overhead to their nests.

Mostly deer, monkeys, foxes and peacocks inhabited the forest on the mountain. Monkeys came to his hut sometimes in search for food. Flocks of sparrows, and doves came too. He loved to watch the herds of mountain deer grazing on the green pastures and sat beside the lake for hours to watch the fishes playing fearlessly in the emerald green water.

Sometimes the village folks would come to cut grass for their cows; or to collect dry branches of the pines, which they used to make fire. They looked at the young ascetic with awe and admiration. He looked utterly disinterested with the things and people around him.

Along the grassy meadow beside the lake, colorful flowers blossomed. Sunlight danced on the leaves and sparkled on the water. Dev strolled on the shore of the lake in the afternoon. When the Sun went to set the sky would be tinged with its crimson hue. Flocks of birds flew overhead to their nests in the forest.

In the deep silence of the mountain, Dev listened to the sound of his breath. He found his breath being subtler and smoother as he kept focusing on it day and night.

Once he asked his Master if he needed to practice a mantra.

"Breath is the most ancient mantra the Self is chanting day and night." His Master said, "Don't doubt in its power. Breath itself is Om, the mantra of cosmic Prana."

"I'll love to chant the sacred 'Om' sometimes, if you say." Dev said. "It makes a very soothing impact on me."

"Do it often, if you like." The sage said. "Om is indeed our very Self. It is that unborn and undying essence within you."

"Is my breath sacred too?" Dev asked sincerely.

"Indeed it is! Breath keeps flowing within you and me and all beings in this cosmos carrying within its bosom the ancient one Life, the sacred and glorious Om."

The sage taught him a secret breathing technique for youth and longevity. "The breath is the secret of life and death, for youth and longevity. Everything depends on how you breathe." He said again and again.

Dev was fascinated to learn the secret of his breath which he thought was so ordinary. "People take their breathing for granted, you know, and they pay little attention to it," his master said, "while the quality of our lives depends on it."

Dev learned to breathe more deeply and fully. He learned a special technique of withholding his breath for a while to elongate his breaths, so he could breathe a fewer breaths in a minute. "Our life spans are specified by the number of our breaths, you know." His master told him. "If you can naturally reduce the number of your breaths you take in a minute, you'll live longer."

Mastering the breathing techniques, Dev sat in meditation for long durations, oblivious of the world outside. He was trying hard to have that powerful experience of extraordinary peace that happened to him at the presence of his Master on the second day of his arrival on the mountain; but he failed to have it again, however he persevered.

Days and months passed, and the young ascetic did not take any notice of that. The fresh enthusiasm and euphoria of the earlier days started to evaporate as time flowed by. His dissatisfaction was growing. He used to roam listlessly among the trees on the mountain. His heart kept swelling with emotions and memories of his past.

On the Razor's Edge

Dev was brooding over his fortune sitting beside the clear mountain stream. It has been more than three years since he came here on the mountain.

Nowadays he feels very restless. Memories come back with a vengeance. He is much bothered when he remembers Lila. Her thoughts have not left him in spite of his desperate effort to put them aside.

Dev tries hard to forget them so he could concentrate one-pointedly in his quest. But memories are not so easy to forget. His head hurts as he tries hard not to think about her. The fond memories of her smile and her tears were making him crazy. She has started appearing in his dreams.

Why did he ever need to leave her? Dev wondered. Wasn't it solely to satisfy his egoistic ambition and selfish drive? His heart ached at the thought.

But he wasn't the one to give way to his unruly thoughts after coming this far. With strong resolve Dev pushed those thoughts aside and sat in lotus pose. He tried to meditate. But his mind was so restless that he couldn't focus his mind at all. He strolled back to his hut.

As he was about to enter his cottage, Dev was startled to find a woman inside. He cleared his throat to make his presence known. She looked back. The face looked familiar. But Dev couldn't remember her name.

"I'm Bella; remember me?" She said.

"Sure!"— Dev mumbled. He suddenly recognized her. She is that friend of Lila. — "Please be seated." He said courteously.

She didn't take her seat. She appeared somewhat perturbed.

"I've come to know your mind about my friend." She said in a cold voice.

Dev kept silent for a while. His head slumped. He took a deep breath to collect himself.

"I love her." He said faintly.

"No; you never have loved her, really," she said, with fire in her eyes.

"Don't say that please, for God's sake!" His voice trembled. "I love her..."

"Wonderful love indeed that made you leave her!" She sounded sarcastic.

Dev kept quiet. He was helplessly searching for words.

"She loved you with all her heart and you didn't care!" She said again. "You've taken an undue advantage of her innocent love."

He shook his head in frustration.

"Only God knows how deeply I love her." He said in desperation. "You are mistaken."

She smiled in derision.

"Am I?" She said sarcastically. "Then will you please enlighten this stupid lady the reason of your decision to leave her?"

He looked up to her and ran a hand through his unkempt hair. "I know you won't believe me and I don't ask you either." He mumbled. "But I've survived here so long, only because I love her and yarn to go back to her."

"Really?" She was ruthless and blunt. "Then who prevents you from going back to her now?"

Dev kept silent. He didn't have an answer. It was impossible to explain to her his present state of mind. How can he with all his dignity go back to his beloved after this failed search?

"You've chosen this path for yourself, Sir; and she is suffering for no fault of hers." She said again.

"I know it. I'm to blame for whatever has happened." He said despondently.

There was stern silence on the other end.

"How's she?" He asked with a slight hesitation. His voice trembled.

"You surely don't deserve to know that, Sir."

Dev kept quiet. Bella was right, perhaps. He has acted irresponsibly to come here in an unknown quest. A heavy sigh came out of his heart.

She noticed it. Her eyes became kinder. "She is miserable without you, Sir." Bella said with a sigh. "Go back to her soon, or you may lose her forever... His Majesty is impatient to get her married, and in case you don't know, there is an open proposal from the King of Pandas begging her hands for his son."

The thought of her marrying someone else hurt him more than he would ever admit, but being too much of a gentleman he chose to say nothing.

A lump was forming inside his throat. He could not say a word.

Bella left after a while. Dev escorted her through the mountain path to the carriage waiting at the foot of the mountain.

"Lila doesn't know I came here, Sir." She said before leaving, smiling piteously, "She'll kill me if she knows. She never wants to be a hindrance on your path, you know."

Dev was feeling miserable after Bella left. His restlessness knew no limits. "She is miserable without you..." Her words were ringing in his ears.

Doubts came creeping in to his heart. Wasn't he wasting his time and youth willing to know the unknowable, to attain the unattainable? A shiver ran through him.

The uncertain course of his life was overwhelming him. He was feeling confounded at his present state of affairs. But he couldn't see a ray of light. If he went back to Lila would she be happy? Will she accept him with the same love and respect? Even if she does, how would he reconcile himself to his new reality? Won't his whole life seem like a waste after this unsuccessful search? What is the use of clinging to such a life? It's better to die than living such a deplorable life.—

A shudder went through his spine. Was he contemplating a suicide? Oh God, what was the way out of this mess he has woven around him?—

Dev decided to confess his worries to his Master. He had deep trust in this wise, old man; maybe he could sustain him through such dark hours of doubt and self-pity.

The sage listened to him intently. He always kept a watchful eye on the boy. He knew what a wonderful promise he held within him.

"Just before the sunrise lies the darkest part of the night, Dev," he quipped.

"How long must I wait, revered master, before I see any ray of light?" Dev asked dejectedly.

"Keep patience, my son." The sage whispered. "The path of self-discovery resembles a razor's edge, you know; but, at the end waits supreme satisfaction and ultimate peace."

"Can I ever do this, revered Master?" Dev said in agony. His shoulders slumped in frustration.

"You surely can do it, Dev." The sage patted him on his back. "It's your destiny. Don't ever lose your heart. Be brave like a soldier, my boy."

There was something in his words that revived and recharged Dev with new zeal. There was no leaving the path without giving it a last try. Dev decided to persevere in his search.

##

Dev resumed his search mastering all his resolve. He persevered day and night. Gradually the memories of his village and his parents turned pale, like the pale pictures of an old album. The memory of his life in the city too was falling away. Only one memory didn't leave him. It was the memory of his beloved. Her memory came to him often like a sweet dream of a distant past.

The Sun browned his slender form and he grew beards. Sometimes he looked at his face reflected in the water of the lake, and could not recognize himself with his dishevelled hair and long beards.

Shyam used to come once in one or two months, and sat near the sage in heavy heart. Dev was changing fast; he could see. He was no longer the zestful youth he met years before. He became unusually quiet and reserved.

When Shyam took leave from the sage Dev used to accompany him down to the mountain. But it was like a routine. Both of them spoke very little on the way. His withdrawn attitude made Shyam worried and anxious. He concealed his worry from the King so far. But if this continues for long, he must confide it to the King; he thought.

The Dark Night of the Soul

There was a cliff at the edge of the forest on the mountain. Beneath the cliff was a small grassy expanse. It was his favorite spot for his morning meditation. The place was very solitary. It was absolutely silent except for the twitter of the birds.

Dev was sitting on a piece of rock after his meditation was over. He sensed a rustle in the bushes at a distance, and an exquisitely beautiful fragrance came to him. It was a heady scent, the like of which he had never known. Curious, he looked around, willing to locate the source of the fragrance.

Suddenly, he spotted a deer at a distance. It came running out of the shrubs and halted there, gazing at him. Just for a few seconds it stood there and then it turned around to disappear in the bushes. The fragrance faded away as the deer was gone.

Dev was astounded to realize that it was the famous musk deer of Himalaya. This wonderful fragrance is emanated during their love-time in the mating seasons; he knew. It comes from the musk pod situated at their navel. Dev was surprised and delighted at the sight of the deer.

He remembered, once his master told him the fable of musk deer to expound the nature of the spiritual search of humans. The musk deer runs hither and thither in search of the scent that emanates from the musk pod rooted in its own navel.

"It has a similarity with us, humans, you know." His master said. "We too go on searching for bliss here and there, while we have it all the time within us, inside our own being."

"Bliss is the fragrance of the Self." Sage Ramanam often said to him.

Then why did it seem to elude him for so long? Dev wondered. "If bliss is inherent within our being, why are we so ignorant about it, revered Master?" He asked the sage.

"It is hidden within you, Son, under the restless chatter of your mind, behind the false selves you have spun around you." The sage said.

Dev was feeling very frustrated. With all his effort throughout these years he could not have a single glimpse of his blissful self.

Dev was pondering his Master's words. "In any blissful experience of life, before bliss happens to us, we're intensely involved in the present moment, you know." His Master says. "That makes the thoughts almost stop, and that brief state of no-thoughts brings up the bliss within us."

His Master is right perhaps. But thoughts were storming in his mind. How could he stop them?

Presently the fragrance of the musk made him more restless. It was driving him crazy as it brought back the fond memory of his sweetheart.

Passion came to rage in his heart like a storm. The memory of that sweet, innocent face and those oceanic eyes made his heart catch fire. They haunted him to his wit's end. Dev was feeling an intense urge to flee back to her and hold her close to his bosom. He was thirsty to kiss those soft quivering lips. He knew how she would blossom in his love. His whole being was stirred by the longing to amend his years of neglect.

Never in his life had he been so much tormented by his mind. With all his might he tried to drive those thoughts away and his head ached.

A sense of deep dissatisfaction and worthlessness crept in to his mind. How many days had passed since he came? He wondered. He failed to find the stillness and peace he desired so much. He was surely wasting his time here. It is better to go back to Lila and live an inconspicuous life with her. In sad steps, Dev sauntered back to his hut.

In the evening, the sage was sitting in front of the cave. Dev went to him and bowed down silently. Every day the sage used to sit on his mat for long hours. He was a man of few words, but his silence seemed to radiate a mysterious halo around him. The halo was made of peace, love and joy. How many times Dev went there just to sit silently near him, and drink the blissful energy he radiated.

But today his mind was restless. Today he seemed to be on the brink of despair. As he stood near his Master, the sage smiled kindly, as if knowing his state of unrest. "Come on, my son", he said affectionately. "You look much disturbed today."

"Perhaps this path is not for me, Master." Dev said despondently. "Looks I'm not destined for self-knowledge and peace."

The sage looked at him in a penetrating gaze. "I know you better than you know yourself, my son." He said affectionately.

Dev kept quiet. He was feeling guilty of disheartening his master. How much he owes to this old man for his support, guidance and wisdom. He should not fail him.

"I'm telling you where you are stuck, my son." The sage said again, startling him. "The very desire for emulating your previous experience is creating the barrier for you. Abandon that desire and you will find peace."

Dev was stunned to learn this. At the same time, he was wondering how the old man would ever know about this — his lofty experience and his struggle to find it again. He had never told him about that. He smiled diffidently without saying anything.

"The supreme state is a state of perfection, Dev." The sage kindly said to him again. "Desire, however noble, is a state of lack— a state of imperfection. Abandon all desires, even the desire for perfection and rest in your original peace."

Dev realized the futility of his egoistic desire to have spiritual experiences and insights. He realized the folly of his incessant desire to repeat his extraordinary past experience. He bowed down to his Master, grateful in his heart for pointing out his mistake.

The company of the sage and his peace pacified him and Dev felt a serenity coming over him. Going back to his hut he meditated till late in the night. Letting go of his desires, he learned to abide in a non-expectant state, loosely floating on the wings of his breath. He was feeling at peace with himself.

Meditation became a very pleasant experience for him. The next evening when he was meditating, Dev found a strange golden egg between his eyebrows. It was the one he encountered at the beginning of his search! Dev was thrilled. The a bright golden-white aura surrounding the golden egg was expanding, gradually engulfing everything in the cosmos…

Dev suddenly felt a strange fear overwhelming him. He shivered and opened his eyes, awestruck, and the golden egg disappeared. Dev felt extremely annoyed with him. The light was soothing and peaceful. What was the fear for? Was it a clinging to his small ego self? Did he resist the extinction of his ego self?

Dev related his experience to his Master. The sage was delighted to hear that. "Fear is natural, you see," He said. "Our shadow selves always live in fear. Only the real Self is fearless, because it is immortal."

"Then what should I do if fear comes?" Dev asked candidly.

"Do nothing. Just trust on God." He said. "Trust your inner guide, your highest self. Everything will be taken care of."

"So, I shouldn't worry."

"No; you shouldn't." The sage assured him. "Just don't resist anything. Flow with whatever comes."

Dev thanked his Master. He felt very grateful to this wise old man.

The Illumination

Meditation became a consuming experience for him. He spent most of his time meditating. During the hours of meditation, a tiny blue dot started appearing between his eyebrows. It looked alive. It gradually increased its size and illuminated everything within and around him.

Dev was fascinated with this vision. His mind was happy and contented as he perceived this brilliant blue light in meditation. He began to experience a new kind of blissful Samadhi.

One evening while meditating inside his cottage, suddenly he felt that he didn't have a solid body. He was fully aware of himself, suspending in a state of stillness. Dev felt a strange sensation of bliss at not having the solidity of a form. He felt like going beyond pleasure and pain, hunger and thirst.

The bliss lingered for a while and he felt light in his body and mind even after he came back to the normal consciousness. This experience made him understand that solidity of his form was really an illusion created by his senses and the mind. If his body really was solid it couldn't have vanished even for a moment, while he was perfectly aware of his presence.

The words of his masters were so true. He thought.

Many strange experiences followed. They came in spite of his not searching for them. Actually they came because no more was he searching for them.

He was lying on his cot one night and suddenly he found his own body lying there, as he seemed to watch it from outside. It was a weird experience.

The very next day he experienced a soothing light expanding from the centre of his heart that covered everything in his room and then melted in to the space.

These experiences gave him the glimpses of his formless nature; but still, somewhere in his mind, there were remnants of the memory of his old self, which existed in the form of his present body.

He couldn't grasp the idea of his infinite being. However, he didn't bother about that. Experience has taught him that everything happens in its own time. There was no use to hurry.

It was about the end of his fifth year on the mountain. He was fairly happy to be able to abide in the exalted states of consciousness for longer durations. But he was also feeling stuck sometimes because he didn't seem to make any further progress. The reality of his formless essence remained a riddle to him.

He confided his worry to his teacher.

"Bondage and liberation are mere concepts, Dev." His teacher said. "They exist in your mind only. Rest in peace as the pure 'I am'- consciousness."

"But that's what seems to be most difficult for me, revered Master," Dev said in despair. "I have tried to abide in my "I am"- consciousness; but, the concept of that 'I am' is always felt as my bodily form, you know," he confided.

"Well, which form comes to your mind when you think of yourself?" The sage inquired smiling; "Is it the form of the handsome youth that came to Sage Ramanam, or is it your present form that looks like a forest ascetic?"

Dev thought for a moment and said, "Surely the form that came here years ago, because I haven't seen myself in a mirror since I came here."

"Well, now you can see it for yourself, dear." The sage smiled. "Your bodily form is just an image of your 'I am'. The image has changed; but you still identify with the past image."

"So we just wrongly identify with one of our images?"

"Yes!!!" The sage said. "It always happens, you know. The images keep changing but your real 'I am' never changes. Behind this screen of 'I am' lies the nectarine silence of peace and blessedness."

"But, how to break away from the identification with the body?" asked Dev. "It is too deep rooted, to be eliminated," he said in despair.

"You just need to know that you are formless and infinite. Live as the formless presence that you really are."

The sage exhorted him to cross the boundary of his limited thoughts and visions. "You know what? You are limited, only by your thoughts." He said. "In reality, you are an infinite being. You are eternity living the dream of temporality. You are the light of emptiness manifesting through this portal of dense physical matter."

The words of the sage kept ringing in his ears. Dev persevered day and night with all his concentration and will put together. "The clue is," the sage repeated again and again, "stop seeing yourself as a limited being trapped inside a body. You are limitless consciousness."

"I intuitively understand what you say, revered master." Dev said introspectively. "But still I feel myself as a being trapped inside the space and time, you know."

"The idea of space and time are also woven within your consciousness." The sage said. "The true essence of your 'I Am' is like pure space. Still, it is not a physical space. You, as the pure consciousness, are really beyond space and time, you know."

Encouraged by his Master's exhortation, Dev renewed his zeal. He kept at it day after day from sunrise till past midnight. There would be days he did not cook at all. He lost all interest in cooking or doing anything for the upkeep of his body. The kind-hearted simple villagers admired the sage and his young disciple. They used to bring enough food for both of them. Dev learnt to forego his evening meal. The whole evening, he sat in meditation, sometimes up to late in the night. Days, months and seasons passed.

When Shyam came to his hut, he would be worried to find the bundle of grocery intact. Dev used to smile at his mild reproach for not cooking the food for himself. He started distributing the grocery items to the villagers that brought food for them.

His form became slender. Shyam felt distressed to see him live like an ascetic. However, he could see something unusual going on within this young man. His countenance often beamed with a strange glow and his eyes shone like stars.

Seasons kept changing on the mountain. After the rainy season was over, the trees and shrubs became more alive and green. The Sun shone bright again.

Dev was feeling lighter at heart these days. The burdens of his past seemed to have fallen from him. He started having the vision of a wonderfully luminous ball of light. Sometimes he would smell a divine fragrance around him. He would feel great joy and rapture in his meditation.

Autumn came with all its splendor of blue sky and colored leafs. A strange cool breeze began to blow on the mountain. It whispered with the trees tinged with red and orange.

Dev was sitting on his cot in the evening. Moonlight entered his hut through his small window. Looking at the moon he could tell that it was the eight day of the bright lunar fortnight. The soft light of the moon covered the hills and valley under its misty blanket.

Dev meditated in his hut for long hours before he drifted off to sleep. He had a strange dream that night; shortly after that he had another dream and then, another. He had a series of five remarkable dreams in each of which he was given a glimpse of a different existence. Each presented him as a personality utterly unlike his present one.

In his dreams, he found himself in different bodies, in different circumstances. In one of the dreams he found himself as an old man, the village priest Vipra, living in a village with his wife and children; then in another, he found himself as a warrior preparing to go for a battle; his sister was putting an auspicious mark of sandalwood paste on his forehead. In yet another, he found himself as an woman — Mallika was her name — the wife of a soldier, crying over the death of her husband on the battlefield. The next one showed himself as a recluse, the ascetic Srinatha, living alone on a narrow cottage, studying the Vedas and Upanishads; and in the last one, he found himself as a King, the King Aditya. He found himself sitting on his court, surrounded by his ministers and generals. King Aditya had a very cordial relationship with his old father, the erstwhile King Sridhar, and he was very happy with his wife, the Queen Shubha. In all of these dreams, Dev lived the lives of his dream characters and their life-stories in its minutest details.

When he woke up in the midnight he felt dazed. He could not quite make out who he really was. Was he the King Aditya? Or the soldier Chitta, or the village priest Vipra? Or was he the ascetic Srinatha? All of them looked very different from one another, but something was common in them...a common chord— he didn't know what it was... However, somehow in his heart, he knew for certain that each of them was him... in a strange way... Even that woman, the soldier's wife was none other than him...

How was that possible? He was in complete bewilderment. He is a man and she was a woman! But there wasn't an iota of doubt that in his dream he completely identified with her and lived her sorrow. And it was the same for all of his dream roles. In his dreams, he completely identified with those dream characters. The memories of those dreams and the dream characters were so vivid that they appeared real.

He sat on his cot, motionless, taking time to come in terms with his present existence. He pondered on his life. – Was it another dream? How do you know that it is not? He thought to himself.

In his dreams he lived all the hopes and aspirations, fears and trepidations, pleasures and pains of his dream identities. He had lived the struggle for survival and the pain of death for each of those dream lives. Those dream identities, especially the last one seemed so real and vivid in his memory that he began to doubt his present existence.

Could it be that, his present existence as 'Dev' too was just a dream from which he would wake up to find himself being someone else? He was utterly bewildered. He sat on his bed quietly wondering about his real identity.

His last dream was especially vivid and tangible. He could tangibly feel himself as the King Aditya even after he woke up. He remembered his old father; it was Shyam, he recognized in astonishment. Shyam was looking a little different and much older; His head was all white and his facial features were a little different too. But somehow in his heart Dev knew that it was none other than him. Dev recognized Lila as the Queen Shubha. They are not exactly the same; yet something was very common in them.

Those dreams were showing his past incarnations perhaps. He realized. A faint smile appeared on his lips. Now he could realize the reason why the Prime Minister Shyam was so attached to him. He was unusually affectionate to him even from the first day they met. Dev also felt a strange sense of closeness with him. The bond of affection from a past life perhaps was playing its role in their subconscious minds compelling them to be drawn to each other.

It was same for his strange attraction toward Lila. The subconscious memory of a deeply loving past relationship attracted them inevitably toward each other. They were soul mates drawn to each other life after life.

Does the soul bear the memory of all the previous incarnations? He wondered. Does it carry the love and hatred of past lives even in this birth? Humans gather around one another or become repulsed by someone even at the first meeting following some invisible cause and effect chain working from long-forgotten past lives.

Now everything became clear like crystal. Dev could see that 'I am'-consciousness is the common thread that carries the memories of those past lives along with all its emotions of pleasure and pain. Following the series of his many births and many deaths, he came to be manifested as he is today. Dev pondered on his present identity. Isn't this identity too a memory, an image on the garland of eternity? Surely it is so. —

His sense of a permanent individual identity melted forever, and with it, melted his idea of an individual self, trapped within a form. He was especially moved by the dream where he had been Mallika, the widow of the soldier. His Master rightly says that the Self has no gender. It can manifest as a man or a woman. A bright golden light filled his heart.

Dev sat down to meditate. For the first time in all these years of his spiritual quest, the idea of a body as his identity vanished from his mind. A knot seemed to melt away liberating his consciousness in boundless freedom of eternity.

He became deeply absorbed in the realm of non-dual bliss shining as his real Self. His existence felt like pure space, which contained every thing and every being within it. It was pure love shining as here and now, as the awareness of a perfect emptiness. All the forms and phenomena dissolved in to it to reveal a peace that was boundless and infinite.

Suddenly that luminous golden egg appeared on the infinite expanse of his consciousness. Why did it come again? What was it? Dev became curious. The egg was made of perfectly translucent golden light. It was expanding.

It became bigger and bigger, and revealed its golden bosom.   A scene was floating there in the golden background. There was a beautiful maiden on a horseback, tightly grasping the shoulders of a man sitting in front of her. She looked proud and a little anxious. She was dressed in a white blouse, blue Ghaghara and black pajama. The girl was around sixteen, fair and flawlessly beautiful. The man was good looking too; he was clean shaven and looked well-bred.   His well-built form was dressed in the uniform of a soldier, a sword hanging from his golden waist belt. The man appears rich and aristocratic. They were eloping on horseback.

The scene changed. An old Brahmin appeared. He had sacred thread around his chest. He was cursing and screaming. 'Let her go to hell.' He shouted, furious in rage. 'I'll never accept a warrior as my son-in-law. He belongs to a lower caste.' A middle aged woman was sobbing. The young lady and her lover appeared on the scene again. She left her parents to marry the man she loved. He realized. But he didn't understand what this was all about and why on earth did these scenes appear to him.

Nevertheless the scene changed again on the luminous golden background inside the translucent egg. A beautiful farmhouse appeared. There was a yard, an orchard, and a little stream was flowing nearby. Dev found the beautiful young lady again, sitting on a cane chair on the yard knitting a woolen cap. She was around twenty now. She looked more mature and all the more beautiful. There were many cattle on their barn. Dev found the young man repairing the shed of their barn. The couple appeared happy and contented in their new life.

A flush of golden light brought a change in the scene. The lady was sitting on a cot on the terrace, caressing and kissing a baby on her lap. A strange sensation sprinted through his spine. Gazing intently on the face of the baby, he felt a shiver in his being. It was him! Somehow he deeply knew inside his heart that the baby playing on the lap of the beautiful young woman was none other than him! He took a deep breath and the scene changed again.

Now there were scenes of death everywhere. Dev felt scared. A woman was crying piteously on the death of his child. Another was seen rolling on the ground sobbing. Dev was almost out of his breath. He didn't want to see it anymore. But he was helpless. It was as if his eyelashes were glued forever to watch this never-ending movie.

The scene inside the golden egg changed again. He found them again on the horseback. The beautiful young lady…, his mother, was tightly holding him, then a baby, on her bosom in one hand; with her other hand she was clasping her husband's waist. The baby was crying. She held him more close to her bosom; Dev could feel the warmth of her skin and a taste of milk in his mouth. He heard the voice of the young man. "Don't worry, darling." The man said, "Even if we die of cholera, we'll find a way to save our child."

Worries and anxieties were written on their faces. They were evidently worried for the safety of their child. They left their village in a hurry.

The scene on the backdrop of the golden light changed again. Dev found the young man lying on the bed looking pale and feeble. A man in white dhoti was standing nearby. The young man— now Dev knew, he was his father— took out a small silk-bag from his waist and tried to hand it over to the man in white dhoti, who was a little older than him.

The bag fell on the ground from his trembling hand and gold coins came out of it. Dev was astonished when the older man turned to collect the coins. It was his foster father, Brahmin Vir Bhadra. He looked younger. He bent down to put the coins inside the bag again and returned them back to the young man.

A wave of golden light passed again before his eyes and the scene changed again. Dev found a lady taking him up on her lap and patting him on his back to console. It was Hema; she looked much younger. Dev was made to watch his childhood inside the golden egg. He saw him playing on the courtyard of their house.

The scenes faded away on the backdrop of the translucent golden light. The golden egg was moving round and round and waves of light shimmered on it. Gradually it became smaller and smaller until it vanished in the infinite expanse of a bright blue space in his heart.

A tiny white dot appeared again in this blue space.

He felt that point of consciousness within him growing wider. It grew wider and wider, spreading through his whole body, gradually extending beyond that. His body appeared to have receded into the distance until he became entirely unconscious of it.

He was now all consciousness, without any outline, without any idea of a corporeal limit, immersed in a sea of light, simultaneously conscious and aware of every point, spread out, as it were, in all directions without any barrier or material obstruction. He was no longer himself. He was no longer as he knew himself to be, a small point of awareness confined in a body. Instead he felt himself as a vast circle of consciousness in which the body was but a point, bathed in light. For a long while, he abided in an indescribable state of exaltation and happiness.

After a while, the circle of light began to narrow down and he felt himself contracting, becoming smaller and smaller, until again he became dimly conscious of his body.

Suddenly a deep sonorous humming sound began to reverberate in the hills and valley. The sound felt like nectar in his ears. It sounded like a faraway melody. It resembled with continuous chanting of OM..! A shiver passed through his being. Was it the sound of silence that his master speaks of? He kept on listening to it. The sound was fading away in the forest of the pines to leave a faint trace in the air. He was feeling complete peace and clarity in his mind.

Dev felt the lighted blue space within his heart again. It was spreading everywhere, enveloping the entire universe. It was the light of his eternal being. He felt waves of peace passing, permeating and penetrating him.

Now he realized that the reality of his being has nothing to do with the historical facts about his body. It has nothing to do with whom he was born to, or, where he was brought up. He was eternal consciousness trapped within a form. All the pain and misery of the limited existence evaporated in the great understanding of the Truth. All the shadow identities dropped off him. It was as if he discovered a fountain of eternal joy within his heart. The elation of being freed from eons-long imprisonment descended on his being.

The great expanse of infinity now filled every aspect of his experience. He was immersed in, no, one with, moment after moment of deep peace. After a long time, coming back to normal consciousness, he opened his eyes and looked through his window. He saw the moon tilting to the west.

There was not an iota of unrest in his mind. He was absolutely peaceful and rested. His quest has ended. His thirst was quenched. His mind was free and taintless.

Dev came out of his huts. Clouds were rolling on the mountains at a distance. A pleasant breeze was blowing, carrying the scent of the pines. Dev sat in front of his hut. Suddenly he felt an urge to play his flute. Ever since he came here on the mountain, he never felt like playing it.

He went inside his hut, and took out his flute from his bag. Coming outside he sat on the stairs and put the flute to his lips.

The ethereal music floated in the night air, touching the earth and the sky, embracing the forest and the mountains. He closed his eyes and felt his breath melting and merging with the music.

Whom does the music belong? What is its name? Dev was playing raga Lalit, a serene raga expressing the mood of the early hours of dawn. While he was playing his flute, a sudden flash of insight illumined his heart again.

The ragas known by different names such as Lalit, Yaman or Bhairav, has a different personality each, expressing different moods, seasons or emotions. But there is something common in them. — The music actually emerges from the breath of the flute player. Apart from the musician they don't have a separate independent existence.

Dev was startled at his new insight. It is just the same for us, the humans. Though we exist with different temperaments and personalities, we don't have a separate existence independent of the eternal consciousness that created us. Each one of us is like a piece of music played by an eternal musician that breathes life in us.

Everything is this existence is expression of this one intelligence; it is Love immortal, never-dying, never-born. Dev felt this great love sweeping his heart, making it spacious, open and clear as the cloudless autumn sky.

Dev felt, he eternally belonged to this earth, the sky, the river and the lake; he eternally belongs to this beautiful existence, which is not different from its creator, just as the music is not different or separate from the musician. All is Om, the supreme reality. His restlessness ceased forever. He had come home. He was content, blissful, at peace with himself and at peace with the whole universe.

Shining Like the Sun

The next morning when the Sun blazed high over the mountain, Dev came out of his hut. He looked at the greeneries, at the grayish blue mountain range at a distance and at the turquoise blue sky overhead as if for the first time in his life he was seeing them. He was seeing everything with different eyes. Everything appeared beautiful and alive.

The trees all around looked exquisitely green, pure and fresh. The mountain Nature unveiled her alluring beauty to his newly born eyes of love and wisdom. He was spell bound and amazed to see the beauty of things. A new existence was opening up and a stream of joy was flooding his heart. Dev felt completely drunk with Life. A sensation of happiness and fulfillment was running within his being.

He experienced the light of consciousness in the light of the Sun, in the mountain peaks, in the course of the flowing stream, in the green of the meadows and in the immense spaciousness of the sky.

Dev found the sage sitting in front of his cave, as if, waiting for him. "Blessed are you;" he said with a contented smile, "your long search has come to fruition."

Dev was taken aback. How did he know this? "What do you mean?" He said faintly.

"You know what I mean. Don't you?" The sage chides him mildly, smiling inwardly. Dev lowered his gaze and smiled shyly.

"Your face says it all, my son." The sage said very affectionately. "You have reached the summit of your expedition."

Dev bowed low and touched the feet of his teacher. The sage bade him to sit down. "I was waiting for this day, you know" He said; "my duty is over."

Dev was startled to hear this. But the sage didn't take any notice of it. "You see, this land and its people have done much for the upkeep of this old vehicle." He said pointing at his frail body. "I wished to give them back something in return. You are my gift to the people of this land — an enlightened King who would lead the land to peace and prosperity."

Dev looked up at the sage, stunned. He was at a loss for his words.

"A few months back the King himself came to me along with his prime minister." the sage grinned.

Dev was surprised beyond limit. For the last few months, he hardly came out of his hut. When did they come? He reflected within.

Dev silently gazed at his Master.

"I forbade them to meet you, because, I didn't want them to disturb your concentration." The sage said.

"You've done just the right thing, master. I'm grateful to you."

"Yes. I was closely noticing you for the last few months."
The sage quipped. "I knew that your search is going to
bear fruit before long."

"It won't be possible except for your support…"
The sage didn't let him finish his words. "Stop it now.
Will you?" He said, waving his hand. The old man won't
listen to a word of his praise. Dev smiled and quietly
yielded to him.

"They came early in the morning, you know." The sage
said again, "The King was adamant to take you back with
him. They implored me to advise you to go back to them. I
promised the King that I would myself hand you over to
them, when I knew that you were ready." The sage
grinned at him and chuckled.

"How're they doing?" Dev asked politely.

"Are you asking about Princess Lila?" The sage smirked.
Dev was taken aback. His cheeks grew red. This old man
is…. In his mind he didn't find the right word to describe
this man, whom he deeply adored.

"Hmmm…" The sage looked at him through the corner of
his eyes. "If you're not interested about her then we won't
discuss it further."

'Good God!' Dev thought inwardly. 'He is teasing me!'

"How is she? How did you know about her?" He asked
openly.

The sage laughed aloud. He looked immaculate in his
toothless smile. "They told me about her." He said now in
a sober tone. "Her enduring love is no less a penance than
what you were doing over here, young man. Now go,

marry her, share your knowledge with her, and rule the Kingdom." The old man said. A beautiful smile lighted up his wrinkled face.

Dev lowered his gaze. Thought of Lila and her long-suffering love brought tears in his eyes. He now knew how deeply he loved her; the mere utterance of her name brought back so much emotion in his heart. His heart was filled with joy in the hope of seeing that dear face again, in the hope of being near her, in the hope of having her by his side. Her attraction was obvious. He was impatient to see her.

But he also felt a subtle pang in his heart at the thought of leaving this dear old man. He loved this old man— the man, who encouraged, exhorted and escorted him in the Sun and the rain through these long years. He has comforted his troubled soul and softly goaded him to pursue his search. He had nurtured Dev with the enduring love of a mother and care and concern of a father.

He spoke his thoughts aloud. "With such love and care you have guided me." He said gently, "I am ever indebted to you, Master. Who will look after you, after I leave?"

The sage laughed; "Today you speak like a kid, my son. Who looked after me before you came?" he said with a grin, "God is there to look after all of us; you know it yourself, my son."

Dev kept silent. He was feeling heavy in his heart. Though his heart was pining to meet Lila, the thought of leaving this wonderful old man made him sad.

"We are but pilgrims on this journey on earth, you know."
The sage said again. "Only two more months remain.
Then, I'll leave this body to merge in to my original
essence."

Dev was surprised beyond limit. "What do you say,
Master?" He said in grief. "No. You can't leave us so
soon."

"It is true, son. My days are almost over. My song will
end soon." The sage smiled again. "So, please don't worry
for me. Go back, marry her and do your duty."

Dev knelt on his knees before his teacher and joined his
palm. "Will you please allow me to take you back with
me, Master?" He pleaded. "I'll make a hut built for you at
a solitary place in the Palace garden, I promise."

The sage laughed again and shook his head. "This
mountain has been my home for the last ninety years, you
know." He said in a serious note. "Like a mother she has
sheltered me. I don't wish to leave her in my last days."

"In that case I won't leave you now." He sounded resolute.
"Please, let me be at your side in your last days. Please
don't send me away from you now." He pleaded again,
blinking back his tears.

The sage gazed at him affectionately. He patted on his
head and relented at his request with a smile.

Dev breathed a sigh of relief. But he became somber
thinking of his imminent separation from his master.

"Is she beautiful?" Dev was brought back to the moment
again by the voice of his master. The sage was obviously

referring to Lila. He winked his eyes, when Dev looked up at him.

Dev was startled to find his master in such a light mood. The old man was evidently in a mood to tease him.

"Yes, she is." He said bashfully, feeling his face grow warm.

"Hmmm." The sage tossed a dry leaf playfully. "Then you're in problem. Is she strong willed?"

"She is, but she is very understanding too," he said grinning. "I only got a small glimpse at her personality so far, and I loved it." Dev was feeling light at heart and he loved to be informal and candid with this old man.

The sage laughed. "Good!" He said, grinning, as he rose from his seat. A cool breeze began to blow. He wished to walk inside his cave. Dev rose from his seat too. "She is precious, a blessed soul, you know." The old man said again on a serious note. "Always treat her with the love and respect she deserves. Your love will make her blossom."

"I'll remember your kind words, master." He said grinning. The sage patted him on his back and said, "You two have been soul-mates life after life."

Dev remembered the dream of his past life as the King Aditya and she, as the Queen Shubha.

"I know, my Master. Thank you," He said smiling, as he hugged the old man in gratitude and helped him to retire in his cave.

##

On the first Sunday of the next month, Shyam came on the mountain to visit the sage as he was used to. He found the Master and disciple together feeding the fishes in the lake. The sage looked very happy and Dev looked a completely new man. Shyam was astonished to watch Dev. He looked so different than Shyam was used to see him in the past few months. His transformation was palpable.

Dev greeted his old friend with a cordial smile. He exhibited such calm confidence, poise and peace that are rarely seen among mortals. A strange light was beaming on his countenance that clearly showed his victory over his doubts.

Shyam greeted Dev happily and he touched the feet of the sage. "Come on the full moon day next month." The sage said grinning at him. A mysterious smile was playing on his eyes. "Make arrangements to take your friend back with you." He said again.

"You mean to say I'll… we'll take him back with us?" Shyam said. He was surprised beyond limit and almost beside him in and excitement.

"Yes!" The sage nodded.

Shyam hurried back to the King with the good news. Dev accompanied him down the mountain as usual. Shyam gave a friendly hug to his young friend. "Today looking at you just once, I realized that you have attained the fruit of your endeavor, you know; you shine like the morning Sun." He said to Dev before departing.

Dev didn't hide his happiness. "It won't have been possible but for your constant help and silent support, my friend," he said humbly, hugging him back. "I am ever indebted to you." He remembered seeing him as his father in his past life, when he was born as the King Adiyta and him, the erstwhile King Sudhir.

"I feel blessed to have a friend like you." Shyam said, and happily departed eager to give the good news to the King.

The Return

Very early in the morning on the full moon day Shyam was preparing to leave for the mountain to bring Dev back with him. A messenger from the Palace came running to him. The King wished to accompany him; he said. When it was still dark, they secretly left in a carriage along with some loyal guards. On the foot of the mountain, they left the carriage and the guards, and climbed the mountain up together.

The sage was reclining on a blanket in front of his cave with his eyes gently closed. Dev couldn't still come in terms with the sad reality predicted by his master. He didn't wish to believe that his master was going to leave his body soon. Until yesterday the old man was in good health. In case his prediction fails, he would persuade the old man to accompany him to the city today; he thought. In this old age he needs care and nursing.

But with the progress of morning hours, the sage was becoming progressively feeble. Dev couldn't help worrying about him. Looking at his white hair, unkempt beard and soft wrinkled skin Dev felt a strange affection overpowering him.

The sage opened his eyes after a while, and smiled affectionately gazing at Dev.

"Thank you, son, for the care and attention you've poured over me." He whispered. "My time is coming near."

"I'll take you with me after they bring the carriage." Dev said adamantly.

The sage shook his head and smiled again. "You have realized your true Self, your real Self, my son. Now it's time for you to give something back to the world to make it a better place to live for future generations." He said without taking notice of his words.

"Live alertly and do the natural things the natural way, watching events coming and going. Your ordinary life will be a life divine." The sage said again, and paused to catch his breath. Speaking even this much seemed to be an exertion for his frail body from which life force was slowly departing.

Dev was listening to his Master in deep reverence, fighting back silent tears. His heart became heavy. King Vikram and his Prime Minister were seen at a distance. Two men hurriedly approached the cave. They found the sage lying on the rug, in front of the cave and Dev sitting at his feet. Dev greeted them both joining his palms and they greeted back.

King Vikram and Shyam approached the sage and touched his feet. The sage opened his eyes. On seeing the King, the sage tried to sit up. He appeared very weak. Dev helped him to sit on the rug. The King and Shyam made themselves seated on a large piece of rock nearby.

"Look, I have kept my promise." The sage said to the King. "Rejoice, O King, that you have got a worthy successor to your throne. He is my gift to the land."

The King bowed low to the sage and said, "We gratefully accept the great gift from you, revered Teacher."

The sage spoke again. "He will be a treasure to you and your kingdom—" He said, "a perfectly enlightened future King."

There were broad smiles of consent, happiness and gratitude on the faces of the King and his Prime Minister.

"We are obliged to accept the gift and your blessings, revered Master." Shyam said with joy, the King nodding his consent with a broad smile.

The sage turned to Dev and blessed him keeping his trembling hands on his head. "I'm going to leave my body, my son, to merge with my eternal essence. Do not grieve for me." He said. He was looking very fragile. Dev was trying in vain to stop him speaking.

"Go with them." The old man said again. "Live a life of perfect health, happiness and wisdom. Share your wisdom with the Princess and be happy together." Dev was listening to him trying hard to resist his tears. The sage became silent. Everybody fell silent.

Gradually, the sage was becoming very still and indrawn. Dev could inevitably see a grand life coming to its culmination. Sage Ramanam was slowly withdrawing his consciousness from the earthly existence. An unearthly luminosity and peace shone on his countenance. Gradually, he became absorbed in deep meditation.

Time passed on without anybody taking any notice of it. They didn't take anything the whole day. The food they brought along with them was left in the carriage. Yet nobody was feeling hungry. Shyam kept wondering about this. Yet he didn't feel like talking. The whole atmosphere was charged with a magical charm as if by an enchanting spell cast by the angels.

The midday Sun shone on the sky and then slowly started tilting back in the west. The shadows became taller and taller. Suddenly a heavenly glow shimmered on the fragile body of the sage; it stood for a moment on his glowing countenance and then disappeared, leaving its faint remnant on the lifeless body of the sage.

Shyam checked his pulse after a while, and couldn't find it. He left his body. Nobody was saying a word, as if, afraid to break the peace and sanctity of the moment. Shyam went down the mountain to call the guards and attendants. The last rite of the sage was to be performed.

The Sun was going down very fast. Dev was sitting beside the lifeless body of the sage. The whole environment took an unearthly hue, and a strange glow was seen in the sky. Suddenly he felt an urge to play his flute. Excusing himself from the King, he went to his hut, took his flute and came back to sit beside the deceased body of his master. With tears in his eyes, he began to play the flute as if to pay his last tribute to his master.

The music was very soft and the melody flied around, as if riding the soft wings of a dove.

Shyam returned back with their attendants, who brought a large bundle of twigs to cremate the body of the sage, as was the custom. Just at that moment a fire manifested on the mountain, behind the cave where the sage lived. It caught the dry trees nearby and slowly came near the place where the deceased body of the sage was lying. The fire slowly surrounded the body in a circle, as if to pay homage to him. Then it enveloped his deceased body to take it in its embrace. Shyam drew Dev to a safer distance, taking his arm in his hand. But, the fire stopped just where the body of the sage was, and didn't advance an inch forward, to the awe and wonder of all. It cremated the body of the sage, without them having to make any effort.

The radiant blue flames were touching the sky, as if allowing the gods to pour oblations in that sacred fire. The King and his minister were standing at a distance looking at the fire with awe and admiration. Dev started chanting sacred verses, until his voice choked with tears and he came upon his knees, overwhelmed with tears of love and gratitude for this amazing man who has just turned into a memory.

He put his head down to kiss the ground in deep admiration to his deceased preceptor— the man who took such great care to feed, nurture and nourish his soul to help him realize his truth.

Suddenly, with a flash, he remembered Lila. "All selves are mortal, Dev. Only Love is immortal." How right she was! He thought in wonder; our mortal selves become immortal in the hallowed embrace of Love, which is our true home.

The fire went down and his body was completely burnt to ashes; Dev took the water pot of the sage that was filled with the water of the holy Ganges. He poured it on the ashes, as was the custom. Just at that moment a torrential shower came down from heaven that washed away the ashes. The Nature itself performed the last rites for him.

They were wet in the rain, standing in wonder, awe, and admiration. King Vikram decided to build a temple on the spot in the blessed memory of the sage. Dev bowed in gratitude to the mountain and the forest, who had been his long-standing companions in his search. They returned to the foot of the mountain, where the carriage was waiting for them.

The Union

With her unadorned look and white sari, they said, she looked like Parvati of the story in mythology. Parvati, as the story goes, practiced penance in the hope of being united with Shiva, her beloved. Princess Lila was living a life of penance right in the midst of the Palace luxuries. She won't adorn herself, won't take care of her body and won't play her sitar either. Smile disappeared from her sad countenance and music from her life. Her grandma Maya would gently coax her to eat and take care of herself, but she would seldom listen to her.

It had been a couple of years since her friend Bella left her to marry the man she loved. Bella faced immense resistance from her family because they didn't approve the boy she wanted to marry; but she did not succumb to their admonition. Lila adorned her with all her jewelries before she left. Bella tried to resist accepting those precious gifts but her friend didn't listen to her.

"They have lost their utility for me, Bella." She said, smiling sadly. "You have found your man. I'm happy for you. Please take these ornaments with you to relieve me of them."

Bella wept at her words. She was feeling terribly sorry for her friend. Dev didn't come back and she, her only companion, was leaving. Both of them sat together for long, holding the hands of each other. Since Bella was gone Lila had been left all alone to herself.

She would spend her days in the Palace garden, all alone. She was utterly detached and disinterested in whatever was happening around her. Seeing her sad face and pale look broke the heart of the King.

King Vikram didn't disclose to her the good news of Dev's imminent return in the fear of breaking her heart again, if he won't return by any chance. His child had tolerated much at such tender age; she can't bear more. The King kept a secret of his venture to the mountain.

Late in the night they returned after Dev performed the last rites for the sage. King Vikram returned to the Palace and Shyam took Dev to his residence. The next morning, the King went to see his daughter to give her the good news of his return. Lila was sitting with her grandma. Grandma Devi Maya is a deeply devout woman and a woman of strength; this was where Lila finds a little solace for her troubled heart.

King Vikram entered the room and took a seat near his daughter. "I have good news for both of you", he announced, failing to hide the sign of jubilation and excitement in his voice.

Lila looked up with her sad eyes. There was no sign of curiosity in them. The King looked at her and then to his mother.

"Tell us what you have to tell, honey, but don't make it long," the royal mother said affectionately, "I was about to leave for the temple of Shiva."

"Ma, very soon Shiva is going to bless our Kingdom with a new King." The King said with mischief in his voice.

"A new King?" His mother reiterated his words, puzzled.

"Yes, mom. A new King. I'd like to enjoy my days of a peaceful retirement." He said jubilantly. "I'm growing old, you know."

Lila was puzzled too. A confused look adorned her face.

"Don't make it a riddle, Vikram." Devi Maya snapped.

King Vikram smiled at his mother's reproach. He was too happy even to notice it. "Ma, I'm very happy today, you know." He said smiling. "Our people are soon going to get a wise and perfectly enlightened King on the throne, and me, a worthy successor."

Devi Maya frowned and shook her head in impatience. Lila gazed at her father's face, stunned. She remembered the forecast of the fortune-teller. That was a long-forgotten story. When Dev came in her life, she thought the forecast was going to be true; but she was utterly disappointed. She looked with downcast eyes, trying to hide her tears.

King Vikram was feeling very sorry for his daughter. He gently took her hands in his, and said, "Dev has returned."

These three words made a fantastic reaction on her. A thrill passed over her being. She became very still and tears flowed from her eyes. Happy tears. She couldn't still believe her ears. She smiled shyly after a while, and lowered her eyes. The King patted on her head and left in joy.

Lila embraced her grandmother and happy tears came to her eyes too. "Look I told you, Honey,… he must return." Devi Maya said, gently moving her fingers through her disheveled hair and patting her with her other hand. "The sacrifice of your love can't go in vain. It had enough strength to move the mountain."

She left for the temple after a while to offer her worship and Lila went to the garden, lest he came and returned back not to find her. Her heart was throbbing fast in joyful expectation.

The Prime Minister's house wore a festive look. Flowers and strings of deodar leafs were hanging everywhere. Shyam did not show up in the royal court. He was busy directing and instructing his servants to prepare choicest food for Dev. It was as if own son was back home from abroad. He had stopped wondering about his unusual feelings for Dev.

Dev felt at home in his house. It was like a homecoming. Now he knew the reason for his feeling at home with Shyam and also the reason of their mutual affection.

In his visions, he'd seen him as his father, in his past incarnation. He remembered how affectionate the old King Sridhar was to his son, the King Aditya. He smiled silently watching Shyam's happiness to have him back again.

Dev was pleasantly surprised to find the variety of food and drink served at his breakfast. Shyam, insisted him to taste every item a little. The habit of enjoying so many items in a meal had long left him. Now he was used to simple food in a moderate quantity. However, he yielded to the affectionate request of his old friend.

Shyam kept looking at Dev with obvious satisfaction and admiration, as he ate silently.

"It would be difficult for Lila to recognize you, Dev, with this long beard and moustache," he said jokingly.

Dev smiled and nodded. "I think so. Will you give a call to the barber, please?" He said. Shyam was happy to oblige him.

The barber came; he trimmed his hairs and shaved his beard. There was scented water in the tub for his bath, and fine clothes were kept aside. This was all so different from the life on the mountain; Dev thought with a little amusement.

After taking his shower he came down the stairs to the large living room at the entrance of the house. Shyam was delighted to find him looking elegant and regal in his clean-shaven face, fine dress and stately appearance. He appeared younger, sharper, more alert and more vigorous than ever before. He looked like an image of perfection.

"Now, everything looks alright," Shyam said smiling, admiring his form. Dev smiled back and took his seat near him.

"Today I'm so happy, you know," Shyam said, "and so proud of you."

"It's the same for me, my friend," He said humbly.

"You see, sometimes destiny gives a hundred-fold back than it took away..."

"You're right." Dev smiled. "It's destiny that brings us together life after life."

"Life after life...?" Shyam was inquisitive. "Do you mean to say we came together in our past lives too?"

"Yes my friend." Dev reclined back on the sofa. "Otherwise, what's there to define the bond of affection we shared from the very first day we met?"

"So true...!" Shyam nodded. "I was intrigued by my own behavior..." He sounded thoughtful. "But is there truly something as a past life?"

"Sure!" Dev nodded. "I've seen many such lives in meditation."

"Very interesting..." Shyam became serious. "Did you see something that indicated my past connection with you?"

"Yes, my friend." Dev said soberly. "But it's difficult to believe..." He hesitated a little thinking how Shyam was going to react to his revelation.

"Please tell me what it was." Shyam sounded earnest and impatient.

"You were my father...," he said reticently, "I mean, the father of some King Aditya... King Sridhar was very affectionate to his son, the King Aditya. "

"Good God. That explains many things, Dev." Shyam was excited. "Now I know the reason of my strange feelings toward you."

Dev kept smiling. Shyam wanted to learn more about his experiences. Dev recounted about his life in the mountain and his many experiences. Shyam listened to it, enchanted.

##

In the afternoon, He took her flute and went to the Palace garden, expecting to see her. The Palace guards took a moment to remember and recognize him and saluted him with respect. Dev was feeling a subtle joy within his heart as he approached the Marble Rock. His heart stopped in joy as his eyes got the sight of the dear face.

Lila was sitting on a couch gazing far. Her unadorned look made her look all the more beautiful in his eyes. Suddenly she became restless and gazed around. When her gaze fell on Dev, she couldn't believe her eyes.—Was it a vision or was she really seeing him? She asked herself.

When she was convinced about his real presence before her, tears, streams of tears came running down her soft cheeks. There were tears at the corner of his eyes too.

"How are you, Dev?" she said faintly. Dev didn't answer. He walked over to her and held her in his hands. She was trembling like an autumn leaf in the breeze. Dev pulled her into a hug. She laid her head on his broad chest. "I terribly missed you," She mumbled into his chest. He smiled into the top of her head and kissed her forehead. "I missed you too, honey."

"Now your prisoner has returned to your captivity, Darling." He said again. "Punish him as you wish."

She smiled faintly making his heart stop. It was an unparalleled smile— a smile glistened with tears.

"Lifelong imprisonment is your punishment." She said coyly.

"I feel blessed to accept the punishment, Your Royal Highness." He whispered, tightening his embrace.

He made her sit beside him and took her hands in his. She still couldn't believe her good fortune. She was afraid lest it was all happening in a dream and she would wake up again in terrible loneliness.

He kissed her hands and squeezed them in gentle reassurance. She smiled at this, her celestial face beaming with glad love. Tears shone on her smile like dewdrops shining in the morning Sun.

The two sat silently together clasping each other's hands as if silently sensing and sharing the joy and sorrow of each other, their hearts beating in the same rhythm. He played his flute for her; she played her Sitar for him.

"Teach me, Darling, what you have learnt in your forest dwelling." She said after a while, smiling idly, as if waking up from a sweet dream.

"It's nothing you don't already know, Sweetheart." He said adoring that dear face, "I have realized that wonderful oneness, which you call 'Love.'"

She was gazing at that dear face admiring his handsome form, freshly shaven face and articulate expressions. "I want to know more about that, Darling." She whispered.

"I've learnt, Honey, Love is the secret of Life," he said playing with her beautiful fingers. "It is coursing in our blood through the veins; it is flowing though our breaths; it is sporting in our marrow within the bones. It is the secret essence of this universe."

"Really?" Her eyes grew wide in wonder.

"Yes, my Sweetheart. Love is our real Self, the sacred ground of our existence." He whispered, his hand gently pushing away from her forehead small locks that covered her eyes. "Death truly has no real meaning, you know."

"That's something I always seemed to know, Darling." She said delightfully. "Love is our true essence. We all have been manifested out of this oneness."

Dev was astonished at the depth of her understanding. He watched her with adoration. She was so amazing.

Lila laid her beautiful head on his broad shoulder. She was swimming in happiness just to be near him. She could want nothing more from life. Drinking his words she felt perfectly contented in her heart.

Dev gently patted her on her cheeks. "You know it, Darling, as well as I know it." He whispered.

"True love makes our false selves die, you know; lovers die, only Love remains." She said, gazing at his eyes.

"Fortunate is the man who gets a taste of it." He said, adoring her deeply. "I'd like to know what it's like to die in love…"

"It's like when you play the music, being immersed in it." Lila whispered. "The musician vanishes, only the music remains." Dev sensed a thrill passing through his being.

"You know what? You too could be my teacher." he said, with a soft gaze on her face. "You somehow knew it all."

"What's it, Darling?" Lila asked innocently.

"Much of what I have realized by going through austere spiritual practices." He said, caressing her face. Their close proximity was filling his heart with joy. "I never knew that life's fulfillment lies in melting and dying in love."

Lila said nothing. She pressed her cheek on his arm. Just to sit so close to him was so much of a blessing for her. She was basking in incomparable bliss.

"Do you remember, Honey, what you once said about love?" He said again. "Love itself is immortal, you said, while all forms are mortal. Now I know how true your words were!"

He related to her how he remembered her words as he was witnessing the cremation of the body of his Master.

"I had an amazing teacher, Lila." He said with a sigh.

Lila could perceive that her man has been different in many aspects from his old, uncertain self. He radiated a deep peace, joy, serenity and composure that were almost impossible to avoid noticing.

"Sure! I see the change he brought in you, Darling," She said. "The change is so profound."

"Everything happens to us for a purpose, Honey," Dev said softly, admiring her, in his arms; "I love you more than when I found you the first time."

Even his ordinary words sounded so extraordinary. Lila didn't think she would ever get tired hearing him speak.

"I love you too, Darling." She said blushing, realizing that she was developing a huge crush on her soon to be husband.

"I wish you to be my teacher." He said mischievously. "I want you to teach me the art of dying in Love."

Lila pulled away and frowned at him, trying to pretend exasperation. "No way." She pretended to be somber. "I'd rather become your jailor and I'll make you work hard for the people of this land. I think this is fair punishment after what you've done to me."

Dev could see, she was fighting back a smile. Her world was filled with joy that he has returned.

"I'll crave to be at your service, my sweet Princess." He said reclining on the couch.

"Five years is a long time; isn't it?" she whispered again, pressing her face on his chest.

"Yes. It was really a long, long time." Dev affectionately caressed her head and playfully moved his fingers through her curly hair.

"But this is nothing," she said in a deep voice. "I would have waited all my life, you know, if you won't come."

"I know, Darling. I am eternally grateful to you, for helping me to be what I am today." He whispered in her ears. "Do you know you were my wife even in a past life?"

"Really!" Lila was excited.

Dev related to her how he found her as the Queen Shubha, in his past incarnation, when he was the King Aditya.

"You know what, Darling? Love is the invisible force that attracts and makes us meet life after life." He said. "It's true for every relation we share in this life."

"We're soul mates....?" She exclaimed in joy. "So we met life after life and loved each other!"

Dev smiled. "That's true; Darling."

"Love is sacred, I knew." She uttered in a soft voice.

"Love is sacred, and so are we, Sweetheart. It is Love that manifests as the human forms of you and me, and it is our eternal guide."

"Our eternal guide...?" She whispered, reiterating his words.

"Yes; Honey." He said admiring her beautiful face. "It is our real guide. But if it must take a form to teach me the art of living and dying in love, it is you, Sweetheart."

Lila smiled. Her heart was full to the brim. She felt deep affection and love for this man. Dev looked younger, smarter and more handsome than ever. He truly has left behind his old self, which was shaky, uncertain and restless. Finding his true Self, he was shining as Shiva.

She was glad that she loved him. She loved him more than anything in her life.

Dev stood tall on the grass and looked at the night sky overhead. The clear autumn sky was studded with stars. He looked at the moon on the Himalaya. His search was over. After many births and many deaths, he found his place of rest. He lost his petty self to find himself, his real Self. His heart was completely at rest. The eternal Sun of love and joy was shining in it day and night.

Epilogue

King Vikram Varma, jubilant at Dev's return, was eager to entrust the royal throne at his able hands. Shyam's joy knew no bounds; he was teaching Dev all the subtleties of administration, royal formalities and protocols.

Within a few days, Dev, became adept in every aspect of royal administration. Shyam was feeling proud for him. With his keen concentration, razor sharp intellect and strong will, he would make a very good King; He thought.

The marriage was scheduled and arrangements were made to bring Dev's foster parents from the village Mandira. They were beside themselves in joy at the news of their son marrying the Princess.

When the stars were at the auspicious constellation, the marriage ceremony was held, as was the custom with the Aryans. The wedding garlands were exchanged between the bride and the groom, holy threads were tied in their wrists, rice and rose petals were thrown on them, seven steps were taken around the fire, mantras were sung and temple offerings were made. They gazed full at one another taking the sacred vow of loving each other till death.

The date of coronation was announced shortly after the marriage. On the auspicious day of the spring festival, the royal couple took the vow to the throne. Everybody in the land was happy for their valiant and noble King.

With his diplomatic tact, merit, and kindness the new King won over all, including his adversaries within a short while. The royal couple was very popular everywhere in the country by their simple and down-to-earth attitude. They visited even small cities and villages to inquire about the wellbeing of the common people.

People use to say that they ruled the land like Shiva and Parvati, the divine couple illustrated in the mythologies. They deeply loved and admired each other and they were students of each other, in the arts, music and spirituality. They were, as if, one soul living in two different bodies.

Theirs was a story of an enduring love that never rusts; theirs was a story of a noble search that strived to seek the true meaning and purpose of life. It was a saga of spiritual enlightenment and it was a story of embracing life with all its veracities after realizing the truth.

Thus goes their story in the land remembered and recounted again and again for countless generations. Every lover in the land remembers their story, looking at the range of the Himalaya. Every seeker of truth remembers their story with awe and admiration — a story that became a legend inspiring men and women to love, to live and to find the true meaning of life.

ॐ ௸

Books from Inner Light Publishers

Affirmations and Visualizations

The book provides a number of powerful affirmations that address various issues of life, like health, healing, abundance, money, self-esteem, relationship, work, business and spirituality. Karma-clearing affirmations are listed for changing the negative thinking patterns of mind and planting seeds of success. The book discusses how you can use your thoughts, beliefs and perceptions to manifest success in every situation of life. Inside book there is a wealth of information. You will know:

- How do Affirmations and visualizations work
- How to silence the inner critic
- What are the rules for successful affirmation and visualization and many more ..

ISBN: 9789382123156

Laughing Buddha: The Alchemy of Euphoric Living

The spirit of Laughing Buddha is the spirit of ultimate relaxation, happiness and contentment. This book gives a rare combination of ancient Buddhist wisdom and its practical use in our daily lives in the modern world for living in joy.

ISBN: 9788191026948

Om Chanting and Meditation

Om is our blissful Self. Om is the mysterious cosmic energy that is the substratum of all the things and all the beings. It is the eternal song of the Divine. This book makes the Om Chanting and Om meditation easy to follow, simple to do, and very effective.

ISBN: 9788191026931

We at Inner Light Publishers are dedicated to publishing books that helps improve the quality of human lives. You are welcome to visit us at www.inner-light-in.com.

www.ingramcontent.com/pod-product-compliance
Lightning Source LLC
Chambersburg PA
CBHW031309170626
46807CB00001B/341